YOU CHOOSE

BATMAN

STONE ARCH BOOKS

a capstone imprint

You Choose Stories: Batman
is published by Stone Arch Books,
A Capstone Imprint
1710 Roe Crest Drive
North Mankato, Minnesota 56003
www.capstonepub.com

Cataloging-in-Publication Data is available
on the Library of Congress website.
ISBN: 978-1-4342-9707-5 (library binding)
ISBN: 978-1-4342-9711-2 (paperback)
ISBN: 978-1-4965-0211-7 (eBook)

Summary: The Joker transforms dozens of Gotham
City citizens into laughing (and robbing) fools! In this
interactive story, YOU CHOOSE the path Batman should
take. With your help, he'll take down The Joker's Dozen!

Printed in Canada.
092014   008478FRS15

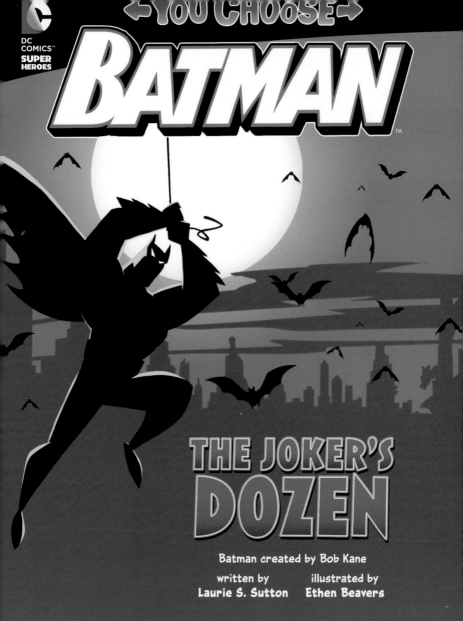

BATMAN

YOU CHOOSE

THE JOKER'S DOZEN

Batman created by Bob Kane

written by
Laurie S. Sutton

illustrated by
Ethen Beavers

BATMAN

The Joker has transformed dozens of Gotham City citizens into laughing (and robbing) fools! Only YOU can help the Dark Knight save the city before the Clown Prince of Crime has the last laugh.

Follow the directions at the bottom of each page. The choices YOU make will change the outcome of the story. After you finish one path, go back and read the others for more Batman adventures!

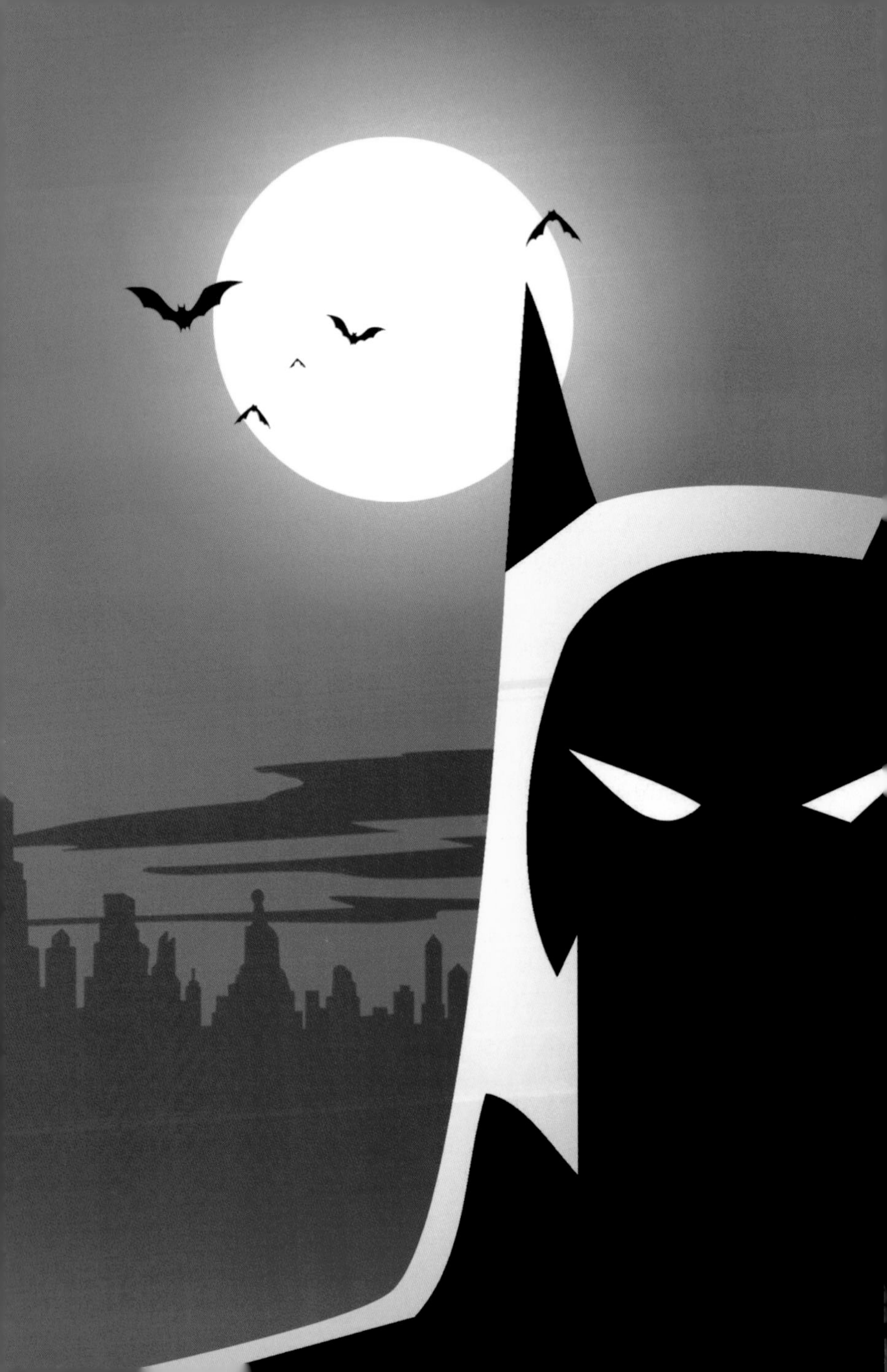

Batman patrols the streets of Gotham City, but these are not the safe streets of the city. The Dark Knight goes where law-abiding people fear to tread, especially after dark.

Tonight, Batman is on the hunt for one fiendish felon in particular: the Joker! The Clown Prince of Crime has escaped Arkham Asylum for the Criminally Insane. The institution's doctors and security officers are experts at handling such dangerously demented criminals as the Joker, but the Clown Prince of Crime has still managed to break out.

"There's no predicting what the Joker will do, but whatever it is it won't be good for the people of Gotham City," Batman mutters as he perches atop a tall building. The hero scans the streets below through a night-vision device.

Turn the page.

Movement attracts the Dark Knight's attention. Batman swings into action! *ZZTT!*

The Batrope snakes out, propelled by a small handheld launcher. The grappling hook at the end accurately catches the ledge of a nearby building. Batman grips the attached launcher and leaps from his lofty perch.

His boots come down on a trio of fleeing crooks. They tumble to the sidewalk, and their loot goes flying from their arms.

"Hahahaha!" they laugh.

"This is no laughing matter," Batman says as he pulls the criminals to their feet. That's when he finally sees their faces.

Batman is confronted by three strange replicas of the Joker! Their mouths are drawn back into grins, their skin is as white as chalk, and their hair is a ghastly shade of green.

"These aren't criminals. They're ordinary citizens transformed by the Joker's laughing gas," Batman realizes. "He's using innocent people as unwilling servants."

Batman ties the threesome to a nearby lamppost as police cars arrive on the scene. Commissioner James Gordon steps out of one of the vehicles.

"That's the fifth incident tonight," Gordon tells the Dark Knight. "The Joker is spreading his bad brand of cheer all over the city."

An ambulance rolls up, and the giggling victims are helped into it.

"It's a good thing Gotham City General Hospital has a supply of the antidote you provided, Batman," Gordon says. "They'll all be back to normal in just a few hours."

"Nothing in this city will be normal until the Joker is caught," the Dark Knight warns.

Suddenly, all the radios in the police cars blare at once. The reports are all the same: there are more Joker-faced crooks committing crimes throughout Gotham City!

Turn the page.

"It seems your prediction is coming true, Batman," Gordon says. "My officers will be busy all night rounding up the offenders."

"That's the Joker's plan," Batman says. "The crime spree is a diversion."

"What's the Joker's real goal?" Gordon asks.

"That's what I have to figure out before it's too late. Knowing the Joker, he has something spectacular up his sleeve," Batman replies.

The Dark Knight launches the Batrope toward the rooftop of a nearby building. He springs upward and disappears into the night.

"Good luck," Commissioner Gordon says as the Dark Knight departs. "I think Gotham City is going to need it."

Batman crouches on a lofty ledge. He doesn't scan the city this time. He studies a small computer screen. The device is linked to the Batcomputer in the Batcave. The Dark Knight keys in commands and looks for a pattern in the police radio reports.

A map of Gotham City appears on the device. Red dots show the locations of the Joker crimes.

Blue dots indicate other criminal activities. Three blue dots stand out to the World's Greatest Detective.

"Hmmm. There's a break-in at the Gotham City Waterworks, a robbery in progress at the Gotham Gem Museum, and . . . wait . . . Bruce Wayne has been kidnapped?" Batman gasps.

The Dark Knight knows that the Joker is responsible for at least one these three incidents. The Waterworks provides the city with all its water. If the Joker tampers with that . . .

The Gem Museum has an exhibit of gold playing cards, including a Joker . . . And although the real Bruce Wayne is Batman's secret identity, someone has been kidnapped.

Batman must choose which crime to investigate — and quickly!

If Batman heads for the Waterworks, turn to page 12.
If Batman goes to the Gem Museum, turn to page 14.
If Batman races to save "Bruce Wayne," turn to page 16.

Batman drives the Batmobile at top speed through the streets of Gotham City. He glances at a computer screen glowing in the cockpit of the high-tech vehicle. A blinking blue dot displayed on the computer map guides Batman to his destination: the Gotham City Waterworks.

"It's time to fly like a bat out of a belfry," Batman decides as he hits the ejector seat button. **WHOOOOOSH!** The Caped Crusader is launched out of the vehicle and high into the sky!

Bat-shaped wings deploy from his harness. As the Dark Knight soars above the streets, he whispers a command that stops the Batmobile and puts it in parking mode.

"The quickest way between two points is a straight line," Batman says as he flies directly toward the Gotham City Waterworks.

The Waterworks stone building looms in the distance. The Gotham River flows up against its steep walls. Large pipes suck in water from the river. Larger outflow pipes expel water in giant cascades.

Batman swoops closer to investigate. A bright flare of light through a window attracts his attention. What he sees is danger.

"Joker!" Batman shouts as he bursts through the giant window like a hawk. He drops from his flight harness and slams into the Joker.

The Joker rolls away from the blow, but he doesn't drop the canister of liquid Joker Venom he is trying to dump into the water supply.

WHAAAACK! A Batarang smacks the Joker's knuckles. The canister bounces from his grasp. Batman grabs the canister and disables it, but the Joker escapes into one of the giant water pipes.

"You've won this hand, Batman, but I have more cards up my sleeve!" calls the Joker, fleeing.

The Dark Knight doesn't hesitate. He pursues.

If Batman chases the Joker down into the sewers, turn to page 18.

If Batman follows the Joker out to the Gotham River, turn to page 25.

The Dark Knight soars above Gotham City in a one-man stealth glider. The Gem Museum is across town, and the little aircraft is the fastest method of transportation. Batman can see the flashing lights of police vehicles on the streets below. There are more deployed than usual.

"The Joker has the GCPD going in all directions tonight," Batman says. "But I'm headed straight to the Joker."

Minutes later, the glider lands on the roof of the Gotham Gem Museum. Batman jumps out and runs to the skylight. He can see the Joker and his gang below in the main exhibit hall. They are stealing the golden playing cards on display, but they're struggling. Each card is six feet tall!

"Those cards are heavy and awkward. Good. That'll slow those crooks down," Batman says.

The Dark Knight cuts an opening in the glass with a tool from his Utility Belt. He measures out a length of Batrope and leaps!

The only warning the thieves have is when Batman slams into their backs.

POW!

The criminals are knocked across the exhibit hall and away from the valuable playing cards. They wobble to their feet, but before they can flee Batman wraps them up with a whirling bolo. They collapse to the floor, unable to move.

"Now, where's your boss?" Batman wonders aloud as he looks around the room for the Joker.

"Yoo-hoo! Over here!" the Joker calls. He stands next to a giant card and waves at the Dark Knight. "How about a game of 52 pickup?"

The Joker pushes the card, and it falls toward the one next to it. Then the next falls and the next, creating a domino effect. The massive cards topple toward Batman.

The Dark Knight is forced to leap out of the way. He tucks and rolls across the exhibit floor. When he regains his feet the Joker is gone, but the super-villain has left a trail.

If Batman follows a trail of dropped gems, turn to page 21.
If Batman spots the Joker's trick lapel flower, turn to page 27.

Batman makes the decision to rescue billionaire Bruce Wayne. The Dark Knight knows that it can't be the real Bruce Wayne, because *he* is Bruce Wayne!

Batman drives the Batmobile to the scene of the kidnapping. It's a fancy restaurant known for its wealthy customers. The Dark Knight sees police interviewing the diners and the staff. He stands as silent as a shadow and listens, picking out important clues from their statements.

"It was that Joker madman," one woman tells an officer. "What a hideous laugh he has!"

"He fed my steak to those laughing hyenas!" a man complains.

"The Joker told Wayne about introducing him to clown fish," another man says.

"There are clown fish at the Gotham City Aquarium," Batman realizes. "It's no laughing matter if the Joker is involved."

The Dark Knight leaves the restaurant and heads for the aquarium!

When Batman arrives at the Gotham City Aquarium, he heads toward the exhibit that has the tropical clown fish. Instead, a cry for help leads him to the orca tank. Hanging in a harness above the tank is the hostage. A giant black dorsal fin circles beneath the man's feet.

Batman launches a Batrope into the rafters above the tank. He swings up to the hostage.

"You don't look anything like Bruce Wayne," Batman observes. He is about to free the man when the harness opens, and the hostage falls toward the water! Batman lets go of the Batrope and dives after him into the orca tank.

"Ha! Wayne was bait for my Batman trap, and you fell for it, hook, line, and sinker!" the Joker shouts. He stands on the side of the tank and reels in the hostage with a giant fishing pole.

Suddenly, a second Batrope shoots upward, and Batman rises out of the tank.

"Oops." The Joker flees with his hostage.

If Batman tracks the Joker in the Batmobile, turn to page 23.
If Batman chases the Joker deeper into the aquarium, turn to page 29.

Batman races into the giant pipe. He can hear the Joker laughing through the darkness somewhere ahead. The eerie sound echoes against the curved sides of the conduit.

Batman pushes himself to greater speed. He must not allow the Joker to escape. Gotham City is in danger as long as the Joker is free.

Batman sees a shape in the distance splashing through a trail of water. The Dark Knight pulls a pair of miniature night-vision goggles from his Utility Belt. He can see clearly now, but what he sees doesn't make any sense. The Joker is spraying a liquid from his lapel flower toward something at his feet. A lot of somethings.

"Rats," Batman growls.

Suddenly, the rodents begin to squirm. Their limbs start to jerk. They squeal as their bodies mutate and grow to enormous size.

"Hohoho! I think that rats hate bats!" the Joker cackles as the transformed rodents race toward the Dark Knight.

The animals swarm over each other inside the giant pipe that is suddenly too small for them.

Batman faces a wall of furry menace. Somewhere on the other side of the writhing barrier the Joker laughs and runs away.

A giant tail whips the air near Batman's head. Claws slash in the darkness. Even with the night-vision goggles, the only thing that Batman can see is a tumbling mass rolling toward him like a giant boulder. Faced with this threat there is only one thing the Dark Knight can do.

Batman does not run. He wraps his cape around his body like a cocoon and drops to the floor of the pipe. The swarm passes over the Dark Knight and continues down the conduit as if he were a speed bump.

"Ultra-strong fabric. I never leave the Batcave without it," Batman says, unfurling his cape. "Now, which way did the Joker go?"

If Batman spots the Joker's muddy handprint, turn to page 32.
If Batman follows the Joker's wet footprints, turn to page 48.

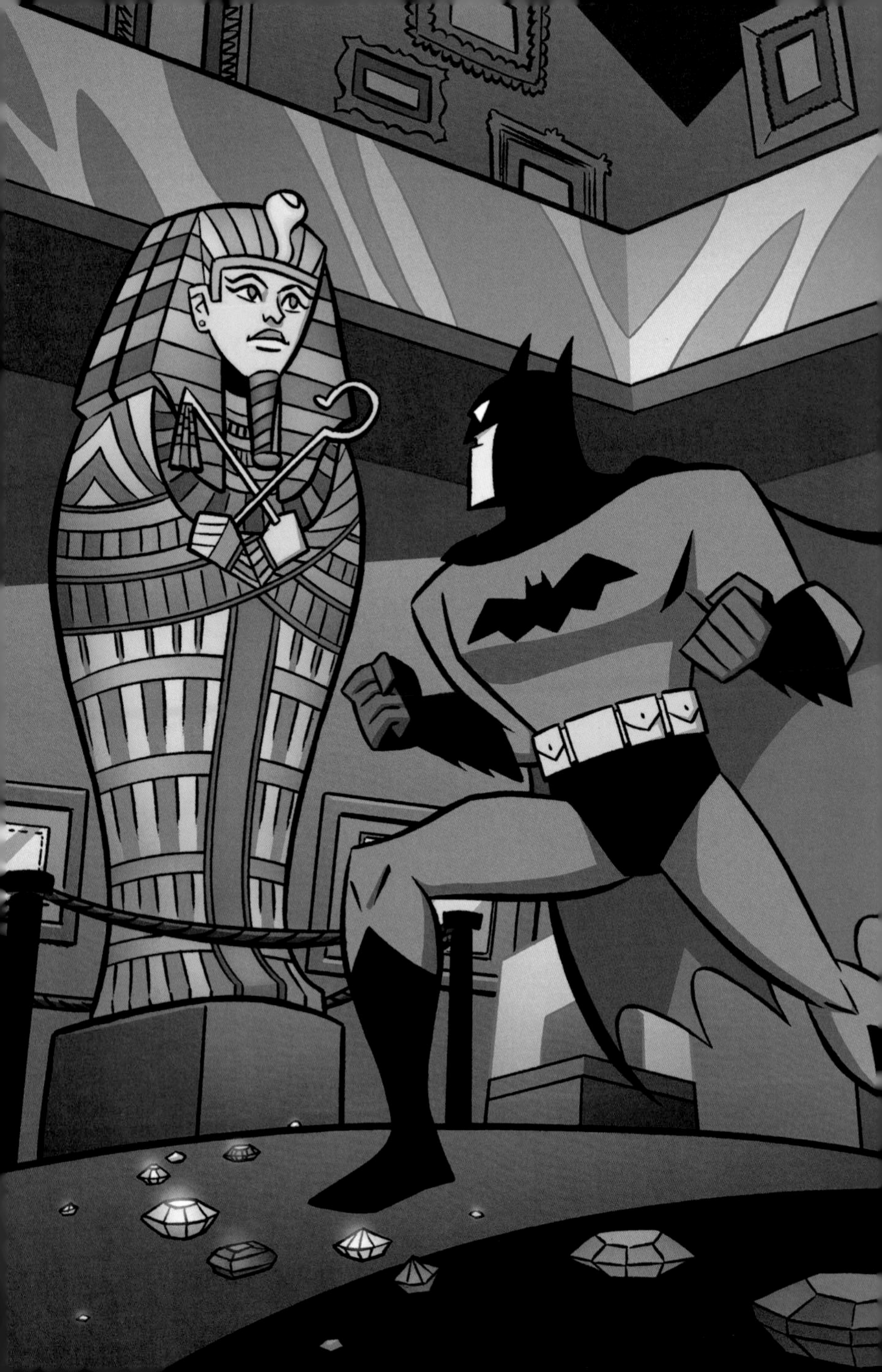

A path of diamonds attracts Batman's attention. The Joker has run away, but he has accidentally dropped dozens of stolen gemstones like a trail of breadcrumbs. The Dark Knight recognizes their special cut and polish.

"These are from the Joker card," Batman realizes. "That villain must've grabbed a few souvenirs before he ran. Well, he's not going to get away with it, not the crime or the stones."

The Dark Knight follows the trail to another exhibit hall. The room is filled with treasures from ancient Egypt. Jewelry that is a thousand years old is displayed in unbreakable cases. A pharaoh's golden sarcophagus rests in the center of the space. The Joker's trail of diamonds stops in front of the gleaming coffin.

"Knock, knock," Batman says as he raps his knuckles on the top of the sarcophagus.

"Who's there?" a voice automatically replies from inside the coffin. "Oops!"

Batman opens the lid of the ancient Egyptian sarcophagus and sees the Joker inside.

Turn the page.

The Joker squirts his trick lapel flower at the Dark Knight and hits him in the face!

"Hahaha!" the crazy criminal howls as Batman staggers backward.

Batman is startled but is not harmed.

"Water!" Batman realizes. He wipes away the liquid. He sees that the person in the sarcophagus is a museum guard changed by the Joker's laughing gas.

"Hooheehaha!" the Joker's laugh echoes through the exhibit chamber. "Hide and seek, Batman! I hide and you seek!"

"I always win this game," Batman says.

"Not this time!" the Joker howls madly. "Catch me if you can!"

"I always do," Batman says confidently.

The Dark Knight knows that the Joker can't resist leading him on a chase. He hears laughter lead one way and sees a shadow run the other way. He has to choose which is the true clue.

If Batman follows the sound of laughter, turn to page 34.
If Batman chases the shadow, turn to page 52.

The sound of squealing tires leads Batman outside the aquarium. He sees the Joker speeding away on a motorcycle. His hostage is strapped into a sidecar. The Dark Knight runs to the Batmobile and zooms after the Joker.

"It's a good thing there's no traffic at this hour of the night. The Joker drives like a maniac!" Batman says. "I've got to stop him before he hurts his innocent hostage."

Suddenly, a hail of small globes launches from a compartment on the back of the Joker's motorcycle. An alarm sounds on the dashboard of the Batmobile and a computer-generated voice warns: "Incoming."

"I see them," the hero replies and swerves to avoid the objects. The Batmobile dodges through the barrage of exploding Joker Bombs.

The Dark Knight escapes that danger but suddenly faces another one. A wall of flame looms before him on the road. The Joker has deployed an oil slick and set it on fire!

Turn the page.

"External extinguishers on full," Batman says.

A light on the control panel blinks, and the Batmobile's computer responds to the voice command.

HIIISSSSS! Clouds of vapor spray from the side panels and wrap the vehicle in a freezing blast of air. The Batmobile passes through the burning barrier safely. There's another surprise on the other side.

Batman steps on the brakes. **SCREEEEECH!** The Batmobile stops at a T-junction in the road. A giant neon sign with two arrows blinks like a kooky Christmas tree.

"I see that the Joker has left a calling card," the Dark Knight says.

THIS WAY! One big arrow points to the left.

THAT WAY! A second arrow points right.

What way should Batman choose?

If Batman goes "This Way," turn to page 36.
If Batman decides to go "That Way," turn to page 55.

Batman chases the Joker into the giant water pipe. It is as dark as midnight inside the iron conduit. Batman can hear the crafty criminal's feet sloshing in the water but can't see him.

The Joker's mad laugh swirls through the damp air. A disk of dim light becomes visible in the distance. Batman knows what it is.

"The overflow outlet. It leads to Gotham River. If the Joker escapes, there's no telling what new scheme he'll hatch," the Dark Knight says as he runs faster. His hand reaches for a Batarang in his Utility Belt.

Batman spots the vague shape of his foe standing at the end of the pipe. The protective grate is broken where the Joker has cut through the metal bars. The Joker turns to face the Dark Knight and laughs.

"Hohoho! Time to go!" the Joker says as he leaps backward out of the pipe.

Batman throws the Batarang, but it misses its target. The Dark Knight reaches the opening and sees the Joker zooming away in a speedboat.

Turn the page.

"He had a getaway planned," Batman mutters as he catches the returning Batarang. "Well, he's not the only one who came prepared."

The Dark Knight uses his handheld launcher to fire a Batrope at the fleeing boat. The barbed end hits the stern and digs in.

The Batrope goes taut in Batman's hands and pulls him after the boat. Miniature water skis deploy from Batman's boots, and he skims the water in the Joker's wake.

The Joker's insane grin turns into a grimace when he sees the Dark Knight working his way along the rope, hand over hand. He swerves the speedboat sharply, but Batman keeps coming.

"Gotta fly!" The Joker laughs as he opens a parasail just as the Dark Knight reaches the boat.

Batman grabs the Joker by the ankle, and they soar out of control toward the Great Gotham Ferris Wheel.

If Batman and the Joker crash, turn to page 68.
If they avoid hitting the Ferris wheel, turn to page 86.

The Dark Knight notices a small object on the museum floor. It rests near the place where the Joker toppled the first giant playing card. Batman walks over to the spot and sees that the item is the Joker's trick lapel flower.

"This must have fallen off the Joker when he ran," the Dark Knight concludes. He bends down and picks up the fake flower.

SQWIIIZZZ! A spray of green gas squirts from the flower and hits Batman in the face. The Dark Knight staggers backward. He turns around and stumbles a few paces forward. Then he stops and sways on his feet.

"Hoo ha ha ha! I can't believe you fell for that old gag!" the Joker howls. He comes out from hiding behind a large marble column. "It isn't often I get to see Batman with a nose full of laughing gas!"

The Dark Knight begins to laugh, but the sound is not what the Joker expects!

"Heh. Heh. Heh," Batman chuckles slowly.

Turn the page.

It starts out as a low gasp, as if the Dark Knight is trying to expel the air from his lungs. Then the sound increases in volume and pitch. "Heh, hee, heeee!"

Batman shrieks like a banshee! The Joker is so startled that his grinning jaw drops.

"My laughing gas isn't supposed to do that," the super-villain states as he scratches his head in confusion.

The Joker watches his foe race around the exhibit hall. The Dark Knight finds cans of paint being used to create new jewelry displays and slathers colorful stripes all over his costume.

"Hohoho! You look like a rainbow, Batman," the Joker cackles.

The Dark Knight ignores the Joker. Instead he starts to steal precious gems from the exhibit.

"Hey! You can't do that!" The Joker gasps.

"Who's going to stop me?" Batman challenges.

If Batman and the Joker team up for a crime spree, turn to page 71.

If the Joker tries to stop Batman's crime spree, turn to page 89.

Batman swings out of the orca tank on the Batrope. He sees the Joker fleeing, dragging his hostage after him. The Joker has a head start, but his stumbling hostage slows him down.

The Dark Knight pursues the Clown Prince of Crime out of the orca section of the aquarium and into the main exhibit hall. A life-size replica of a whale hangs from the ceiling as if swimming in the ocean. Models of sharks and dolphins and penguins surround the giant mammal to emphasize its monumental scale.

As Batman races beneath the behemoth the Joker throws a giant firecracker into its mouth.

BWAAAM! The model shakes violently. The jaw breaks off and falls toward the Dark Knight!

Batman launches a Batrope toward a replica dolphin. The line wraps around the model, and Batman uses it to swing out of danger. His momentum carries him across the exhibit hall and over the Joker's head.

He lands in front of his foe. "Hand over the hostage," Batman commands.

Turn the page.

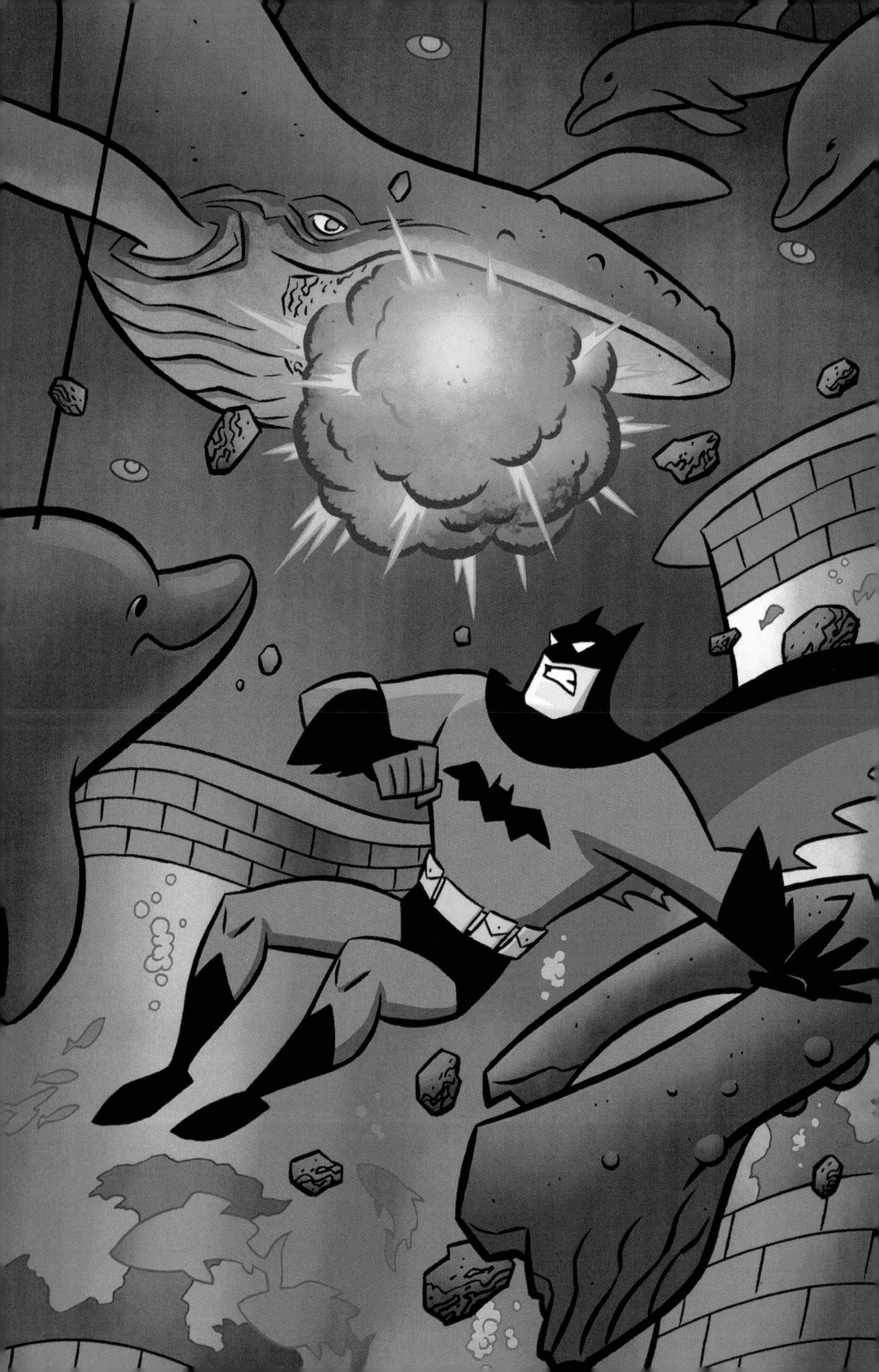

"He was slowing me down anyway," the Joker replies and shoves the man at the Dark Knight.

Batman catches the frightened hostage as the villain flees, laughing like a hyena.

"Are you all right?" Batman asks the man.

"Yes," the man replies. "I told that kook that I wasn't Wayne, but he thought I was joking."

"Everything is a joke to him," Batman says. He pulls a tiny phone from his Utility Belt and hands it to the man. "Call the police and let them know you're okay. I'll take care of the Joker."

The Dark Knight sprints out of the exhibit hall. Suddenly, he hears the sound of laughing hyenas.

"Those are the Joker's pets," Batman realizes. He finds the animals fighting over a strange object. It looks like a dinosaur claw!

"That's what I call an unusual clue," Batman admits. "If I find out where it comes from, I'll find the Joker."

If the claw leads Batman to a movie set, turn to page 73.
If the claw comes from a giant toy, turn to page 92.

The pipe branches left and right, but Batman has trained himself to spot even the smallest clue. An odd speck of mud draws his attention. The sides of the pipe are slick with slime and grime, but the shape of this tiny dab of dirt is like a neon sign to the World's Greatest Detective.

"The Joker's handprint. He must have braced himself against the wall here," Batman mutters. "He went this way."

The Dark Knight follows the Joker's trail through the pipe. It soon becomes clear to Batman that his foe has not tried to conceal his escape.

"Either the Joker is just too crazy to care about leaving a trail, or he wants me to follow him," Batman considers. He grits his teeth in determination. "Either way, I'm going to catch him."

A sound attracts the Dark Knight's attention. The shape of the underground pipe distorts the noise, but Batman recognizes it as music. He follows it and finds an opening in the pipe.

Batman looks up to see an open manhole. The music is coming from above. Along with the music, Batman hears people laughing.

"Uh-oh. Has the Joker's laughing gas struck again?" the Dark Knight asks himself.

Batman launches his Batrope up through the open manhole and leaps upward. He expects the worst, but he finds that he is in the middle of a celebration. People are laughing because they are enjoying a parade!

Batman is relieved, but he doesn't relax. The Joker went this way, and the confusion of a parade is just his kind of camouflage.

A sudden scream alerts the Dark Knight to trouble. A short distance down the street a float veers out of control.

"The Joker!" Batman realizes instantly.

Turn to page 38.

Batman runs in the direction of the Joker's laughter. The sound leads him through the halls of the Gotham Gem Museum. Precious stones and jewelry sparkle inside glass display cases. Batman notices that all the cases are unbroken.

"The Joker must be in a hurry. He isn't stopping to steal anything," Batman observes.

SMASH! The sound of shattering glass echoes down the corridor. "Maybe I spoke too soon."

Batman races into the next exhibit hall and sees the Joker standing in the frame of a broken window. Shattered glass is on the floor.

"It's been fun, but I've got to fly!" the Joker cackles and leaps out the window.

The criminal lands in the seat of a one-man helicopter hovering just beyond the window. Batman reaches the opening just as the Joker waves goodbye.

"Two can play this game," the Dark Knight says as he operates a remote control. The Bat-copter silently descends from the roof.

Batman jumps into the cockpit. The radar display picks up the Joker's helicopter.

"You can run, but you can't hide," the Dark Knight declares.

Batman takes the Bat-copter out of stealth mode and activates powerful rotors. The little aircraft roars to life and flies as swift as an arrow in pursuit of the Joker. Batman catches up to the fleeing felon in less than a minute.

WHOOOOSH! The Bat-copter zooms past the Joker in the night sky. The turbulence in its wake buffets the Joker's helicopter and jars the villain in his seat. He struggles to stabilize the vehicle and almost loses control.

Suddenly, the Bat-copter zooms past the Joker a second time. His helicopter is almost knocked out of the air.

Batman banks his aircraft and makes another pass at the Joker. He knows that he can fly rings around the Joker's helicopter, and he is proving it. He also wants to force the Joker to land. Batman wants his archenemy on the ground.

Turn to page 42.

Batman faces a crazy choice. The Joker has taunted Batman with two ways to find him and his helpless hostage. Only one clue is true. Batman knows he must not follow a false lead.

"This way," the Dark Knight decides.

Batman twists the Batmobile's steering wheel and steps on the accelerator. The vehicle turns left and takes off with the speed of a missile.

"Activate headlights, ultra-spectrum mode," the Dark Knight commands.

The change in the visible light from the headlights is barely noticeable to the human eye, but the Joker's motorcycle tire marks are revealed in the high-frequency beams. They head out of town as straight as an arrow.

"He's not trying to hide his trail anymore. He knows that wall of fire didn't stop me, and he put up that neon sign to delay me," Batman concludes as he follows the Joker's route.

The motorcycle tire marks lead to the Gotham City Amusement Park. Batman is not surprised.

"This is the perfect playground for the Joker," Batman says.

The Dark Knight finds the brightly colored motorcycle parked in front of the Fun House.

"If I know the Joker, he's made this into a not-so-fun house," Batman mutters as he enters the building.

The Dark Knight is right!

A trapdoor opens under his feet as soon as he steps inside. There is a viper pit below filled with hissing snakes.

Batman uses his quick reflexes and a Batrope to avoid falling to his doom. He swings to solid ground but is wary about his surroundings.

"There's no telling what surprises the Joker has waiting for me in here," Batman realizes.

Batman walks forward cautiously. His nerves are tense, and he expects the unexpected at any moment.

CLICK! WHIIIIR! That moment arrives sooner than he thinks!

Turn to page 45.

Batman swings on his Batrope toward the menace. He soars over a line of parade floats shaped like cakes, pies, and other sweet treats.

"This is the Bakers' Day Parade," Batman says. "The Joker is trying to turn it into a disaster."

The Dark Knight lands on the maverick float and sees the Joker behind the wheel. The super-villain is driving wildly and laughing all the way.

"Hohoho! Which way should I go?" the Joker sings out of tune.

The Joker swerves the vehicle left, then right, then left again. Batman grabs the steering wheel and straightens out the float's course.

"Booo! You're no fun!" the Joker complains. He jumps out of the vehicle and onto the float as the Dark Knight steps on the brakes. The crazy criminal climbs up onto the giant replica of a layer cake.

"I'll race you to the cherry on top!" the Joker cackles as he scrambles higher and higher.

Batman sets the emergency brake on the vehicle. He looks up and sees the Joker climbing the layer cake float like a mountain goat.

"Race me to the top? No contest." Batman shrugs as he fires the Batrope. The Dark Knight zooms through the air and lands on the top of the cake.

The Joker looks up and sees his foe waiting for him at the summit of the layer cake float.

"Hahaha! Nice trick! I have a few of those myself," the Joker proclaims.

He then pulls a small object out of his jacket. Batman recognizes it as one of the madman's gas grenades. There's no telling if the gas is poisonous or harmless.

Batman flings a Batarang and knocks the grenade out of the Joker's grip. It sails through the air and lands in Batman's outstretched hand.

"You caught my grenade, but you still haven't caught me!" the Joker says, jumping from the float.

Turn the page.

Batman watches as the Joker leaps into thin air. The criminal reaches for the strings of a cupcake balloon. The Jeering Jester grabs one of the ropes and cuts the rest. The balloon begins to rise into the sky and the Joker goes with it.

"It looks like I get the last laugh! Hahaha!" the Joker giggles as he floats away.

"Sorry to burst your bubble, Joker," Batman says as he fires a dart at the cupcake balloon.

The little projectile pierces the balloon's plastic skin. *BLAAAAAARRRP!* The balloon deflates and flies in all directions.

The Joker hangs on tight until it finally lands in front of a squad of waiting police cars. The Dark Knight jumps down from the float and wraps up the Joker with a Batrope.

"He's all yours, Commissioner," Batman tells Gordon and hands over the end of the Batrope.

"Let them eat cake!" the Joker laughs madly.

"I prefer doughnuts," Gordon replies.

THE END

To follow another path, turn to page 11.

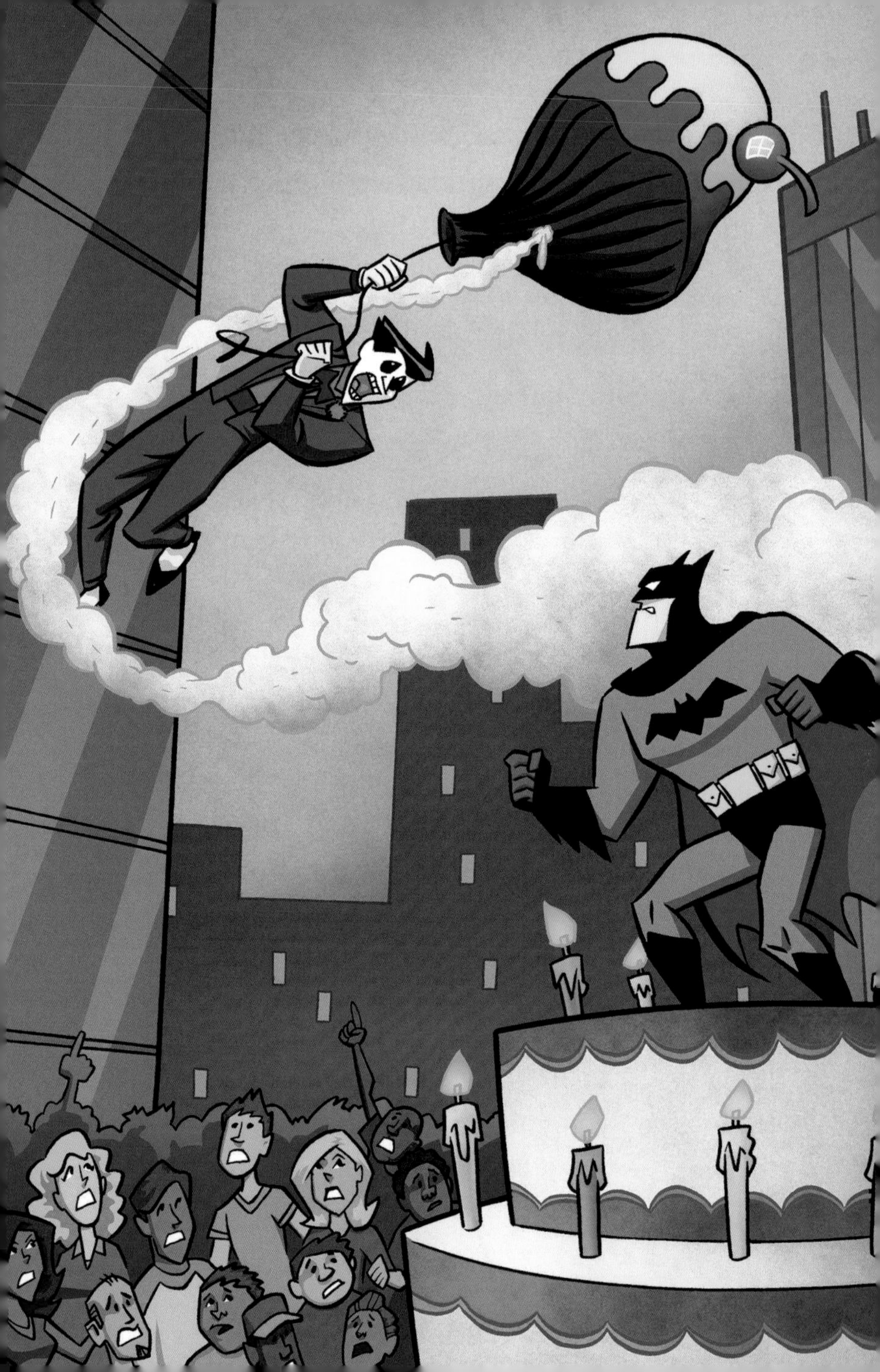

Alarms sound on the helicopter's control panel. Flashing red lights warn of danger and multiple mechanical failures.

The Joker heads for a crash landing. At the very last second he manages to regain some control but only enough to prevent a total disaster. The helicopter snags the top of a mound of scrap metal in the Gotham City Recycling Center and tumbles down the side. When the aircraft reaches the bottom it's ready to be added to the scrap heap.

"Well! Any landing you can walk away from is a good one," the Joker says as he crawls from the wreckage and staggers a short distance.

Batman makes a controlled, vertical landing nearby. When the Joker sees the Bat-copter he realizes what, and who, knocked his helicopter out of the sky.

The Joker grumbles as he runs away. Batman sees his foe fleeing deeper into the recycle yard. Mountains of metal and heaps of paper goods loom in the darkness.

The space between the mounds is wide enough for a dump truck to pass, but not much more than that.

Batman knows that the restricted space is both an advantage and a danger.

"The Joker won't get far in the narrow maze, but he can collapse one of these mounds on top of me," Batman observes. "My guess is that he'll try to take me out before I can take him in."

As if to make the Dark Knight's prediction true, a landslide of scrap metal rumbles down the side of the nearest heap. The Joker's mad laughter rings out in the dark.

"Look out belooooow!" the super-villain howls with glee.

Batman reacts with the speed of a panther. Instead of running away from the avalanche, he races toward it. The Joker watches in wonder as the Dark Knight launches a Batrope straight up into the air.

Then, Batman lifts into the night sky!

Turn the page.

Batman hangs from the Batrope, which is suspended Bat-copter. It is in stealth mode again and is as quiet as a whisper. Batman uses the remote control device to fly the aircraft toward the Joker and knock him off the top of his perch.

POW!

The Jeering Jester isn't laughing as he tumbles down the side of the pile.

"Ow! Ow! Ow!" the Joker complains as he bounces to the bottom.

Batman lands gently in front of the fallen felon.

"Who's the king of the hill now?" the Dark Knight says as he puts the Joker in Bat-cuffs.

"I demand a rematch," the Joker grumbles.

"Don't you remember what I said at the museum?" Batman reminds the Joker. "I always win this game."

THE END

To follow another path, turn to page 11.

CLANK!

The sound of a gear activating is all the warning that the Dark Knight gets. Machinery comes to dangerous life beneath Batman's feet. The wooden floor slats transform into the panels of a treadmill. The floor goes into motion and Batman starts walking to keep up the pace.

"This treadmill is making me walk in place. I could be here forever," the Dark Knight observes.

Suddenly, flames shoot out from the walls! Batman ducks and rolls to dodge the danger. He avoids the hazard, but now he's lying on the treadmill instead of walking. It carries him backward toward the open viper pit.

At the last moment Batman jumps off the treadmill and uses his whole body as a battering ram to crash through the wall.

SMAAASH! He lands in a room filled with a kaleidoscope of Caped Crusaders!

Batman looks around. He is surrounded by dozens of Dark Knights. They mirror his moves.

Turn the page.

"I'm in the Mirror Maze," Batman realizes.

A beam of light strikes one of the mirrors. It reflects to another mirror and another until a web of dangerous brilliance surrounds him.

"Correction. I'm in a laser cage," the Dark Knight amends. "The Joker is setting traps to keep me from rescuing his hostage. He might slow me down, but he won't stop me."

Batman reaches into his Utility Belt and takes out a small can of black paint. He sprays a thin layer on the surface of the nearest mirror. The laser beam can't reflect anymore, and the whole web instantly falls apart.

"One weak link breaks the chain," Batman says.

After that, it's easy for Batman to find his way out of the Mirror Maze. It's not hard to find the Joker, either. All the Dark Knight needs to do is follow the sound of hysterical laughter.

Batman finds the Joker in the center of the amusement park next to a giant fireworks rocket.

He dances around the rocket, threatening to light the fuse with a torch. The hostage is strapped to the side of the rocket and pleads with the Joker to let him go.

"You're going to 'go' all right," the Joker promises gleefully. "Up, up, and away!"

"You've gone to a lot of trouble for nothing," Batman announces calmly as he walks out of the shadows toward his foe.

"Millions of dollars in ransom for the famous Bruce Wayne isn't 'nothing,'" the Joker replies.

"The joke is on you. That isn't Bruce Wayne," Batman says.

"W-whaaat?" the Prince of Pranksters stammers in surprise.

Batman uses the Joker's confusion to throw a Batarang at his foe. A net pops out and snares the super-villain. The torch drops from his hand.

"It looks like this case is all wrapped up," the Dark Knight declares.

THE END

To follow another path, turn to page 11.

The Joker has a head start, but Batman can hear him sloshing in the shallow water draining through the massive pipe. The Dark Knight runs toward the sound but comes to a T-split in the tunnel. He is forced to stop and choose.

Which way did the Clown Prince of Crime flee? Left? Right?

A blob of water drops on top of the Dark Knight's head. He looks up and sees damp, dripping footprints on a ladder leading up out of the pipe.

"Joker, sometimes you are so obvious," Batman mutters.

He grabs the first metal rung of the ladder and starts to climb. It leads to a drainage grate in the middle of the Gotham City Convention Center. The lock is broken, and the grate is open. Batman isn't certain what danger might be above his head.

"The element of surprise always works for me," the Dark Knight decides as he launches a barbed Batrope up through the opening.

Three seconds is all it takes. The barb snags on the open metal framework of the ceiling, and the Batrope snaps into place.

The Dark Knight rises out of the underground like a creature out of myth. He is surprised to hear a crowd cheer!

"Woo-hoo! Best entrance ever! Great costume!" voices shout enthusiastically.

It takes a lot to surprise the Dark Knight, but the sights and sounds he experiences make his eyes go wide behind his mask. Batman hangs from the ceiling struts and looks down at hundreds of super heroes, ghosts, and goblins!

Where am I? the Dark Knight wonders.

A colorful banner hanging nearby reveals the answer. Bold letters proclaim: GOTHAM CITY COSTUME CONTEST!

Batman realizes that the witches, princesses, and monsters are simply ordinary people dressed in costumes. The only danger here is the fact that the Joker is loose somewhere in the crowd.

Turn the page.

Batman uses his vantage point to search for the maniacal miscreant. He scans the crowd for the colorful criminal. Unfortunately, the whole crowd is colorful. The Joker blends right in.

"Be patient," Batman tells himself. "If I know the Joker, he won't be able to resist making a commotion. He'll stand out."

As if to prove the Dark Knight right, an uproar erupts near the center of the convention hall. A man with green hair and a purple suit stands atop a stage.

"Bingo," Batman says.

The Dark Knight runs along the network of ceiling struts until he is directly above the laughing lunatic.

He leaps down toward the Joker!

Turn to page 58.

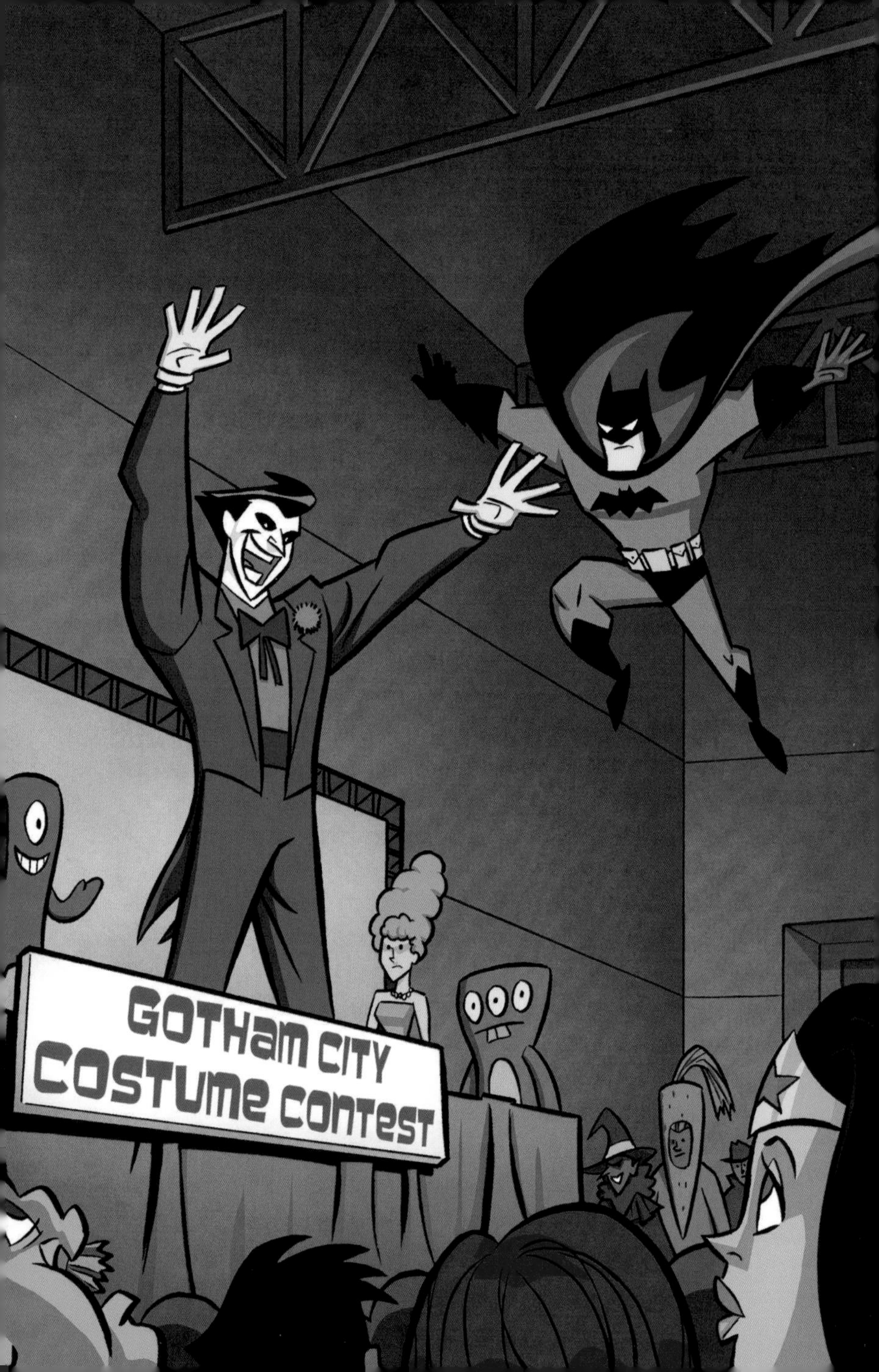
GOTHAM CITY
COSTUME CONTEST

Batman decides to pursue the shadow fleeing down the museum corridor. The World's Greatest Detective knows that the sound of the Joker's laugh could be a simple recording designed to lead him down a false trail. The shadow could be faked, too, but the Dark Knight decides to go after the clue that is moving.

Batman runs down the hallway. He realizes that he's taking a chance that whoever he's chasing is the actual Joker and not another innocent citizen warped by the laughing gas.

SMAAAASH! The sound of breaking glass assures Batman that he is on the right trail.

He reaches an exhibit hall and sees a broken display case. A torn label identifies what has been stolen from the case.

"A jade Laughing Buddha," Batman says as he reads the card. "I'm definitely on the trail of the Joker."

CRAAAASH! The sound of more mayhem echoes through the museum.

"I better catch that maniac before he breaks everything in this place," Batman decides. Batman follows the sound of crashing cases to an exhibit hall devoted to artifacts from the Aztecs and Mayans of ancient Mexico. He spots the Joker with a grinning, golden mask in his hands.

"Who knew the Aztecs had a sense of humor?" The villain laughs and puts the mask on his face.

"It's not a grin. It's a grimace," the Dark Knight informs his foe. "That's a death mask."

"Hohoho! Well, I'd like to think that they died laughing!" the Joker howls.

The Joker uses the mask like a weapon and throws it at Batman. The Dark Knight catches it. He can't let the villain damage such a valuable piece of Aztec culture.

While Batman saves a piece of history, the Joker runs from the hall laughing like a hyena.

"If I can't steal what I came here for, I'll just have to find something else!" the Joker cackles and skips playfully though the exhibit halls.

Turn the page.

"This isn't a shopping mall," Batman declares.

The Dark Knight throws a bolo at his foe. **WHOOOSH! WHOOOSH! WHOOOSH!** The triple strands wrap around the Joker. The crazy criminal tips over and falls to the floor.

"Ow," the Joker complains weakly.

Batman stands over his captured foe. He knows that this was too easy. He suspects that the Joker is up to something.

HIIIISSS! Acid squirts out of the Joker's lapel flower and dissolves the bolo wires holding him captive. The Dark Knight reaches for a Batarang in his Utility Belt.

"Be very careful what you do next!" the Joker warns. "I have a hostage!"

Turn to page 62.

"I have a fifty-fifty chance of choosing the correct clue," Batman says. "I need to increase those odds."

The Dark Knight activates sensors mounted on the Batmobile. The sensors scan for thermal differences in the air. Blobs of warm reds and cool blues appear on a display screen in the cockpit of the vehicle. A stripe of red stands out in sharp contrast.

"That's the heat from Joker's motorcycle engine," Batman concludes. The thermal trail heads off to the right. "He went That Way."

The Dark Knight turns the Batmobile to the right and zooms in pursuit. The Joker's heat trail is not hard to follow in the cool night air. It leads Batman to a group of rundown warehouses. The buildings are dark and look deserted.

Batman slows the Batmobile and cruises between the structures. The thermal trail stops in front of one of the buildings.

"It looks like I've found the Joker's secret hideout," Batman decides.

Turn the page.

The Dark Knight drives past the warehouse and parks the Batmobile a hundred feet away.

"If the Joker is watching, he'll think I've missed his hideout. He won't be expecting me, and I can surprise him," Batman reasons. The hero keeps hidden in the shadows as he works his way back to the building on foot.

The Dark Knight finds a side door, but before he tries to open it he looks for booby traps.

Batman takes a small device from his Utility Belt and scans for electrical activity.

"The door isn't wired," Batman concludes. He switches to a "bomb sniffing" mode. "No explosives detected."

The door appears safe, but then the Dark Knight spots its rusty hinges.

"Those could be trouble," he decides.

Batman pulls a capsule of lubricant spray from his Utility Belt. He squirts it on the creaky hinges to keep them silent as he slowly opens the door and steps inside.

The Dark Knight is prepared for any of the Joker's tricks, but this one takes him by surprise! Bright spotlights come on and illuminate a bizarre scene.

Batman is standing in the ancient Colosseum of Rome!

A crowd roars at the sight of the Dark Knight. He shades his eyes against the light and sees that the audience is just a bunch of cardboard cutouts. They are fakes. The cheers are a recorded loop.

"All hail the Joker!" a different voice declares.

Batman turns and sees the Clown Prince of Crime dressed up as a Roman emperor and sitting on a royal throne. His hostage is tied to a chair next to him. A pair of pet hyenas drools at the Joker's side.

Suddenly, a hatch opens in the floor of the arena. Gladiators wearing Joker masks climb out and surround the Dark Knight.

"Let the games begin!" the Joker declares.

Turn to page 65.

Batman lands on his foe. The Joker is knocked flat on his jeering face. The impact jars the stage and it shudders beneath their feet. The banner behind them falls onto the crowd. The onlookers gasp — then they cheer!

"Hohoho! They think this is a show!" the Joker says. "I'll give them a performance they won't forget!"

The Joker squirms out of Batman's grasp and slides down the side of the stage. The crowd steps back to give him room to land. The Joker takes a bow before throwing a handful of exploding marbles at the base of the stage.

BLAAAM! BLAAAM! The stage supports crumble, and it starts to topple.

Batman launches a length of Batrope. It snakes out and wraps around a nearby pillar. Another Batrope snares a second pillar. There's nothing to stop the stage as it teeters toward the stunned crowd — nothing except Batman.

The Dark Knight grips both ropes in one fist as he slides down the side of the stage.

He hits the floor hard but doesn't let go as he rolls under the belly of the massive stage. When he reaches the other side, he fires a third Batrope into the ceiling struts.

"Up, up, and away," Batman says as he soars toward the steel framework.

The Dark Knight attaches the cradle of ropes to the supports as the stage display finally falls — and stops! Batman pulls on the ropes, adding the strength of his muscles to halt the disaster.

"Wow! Who is that guy? He's the greatest!" the guests exclaim.

"Heeheehee! We haven't reached the final act of this drama!" the Joker howls. He runs across the tops of tables filled with contest trophies.

A bolo whirls through the air and wraps around the fleeing felon's ankles.

"Looks like we have a winner!" Batman states from above.

The Dark Knight slowly descends from the shadowy realm of the convention hall ceiling.

Turn the page.

The crowd cheers loudly at his appearance.

The Joker struggles to his feet and tries to flee. His ankles are bound by the Bat-bolo, so he hops toward the nearest exit. He does not get far.

The Joker tips over and falls into a megasized costume contest trophy. Batman steps forward and reads the caption etched on the trophy: "Best in Show."

THE END

To follow another path, turn to page 11.

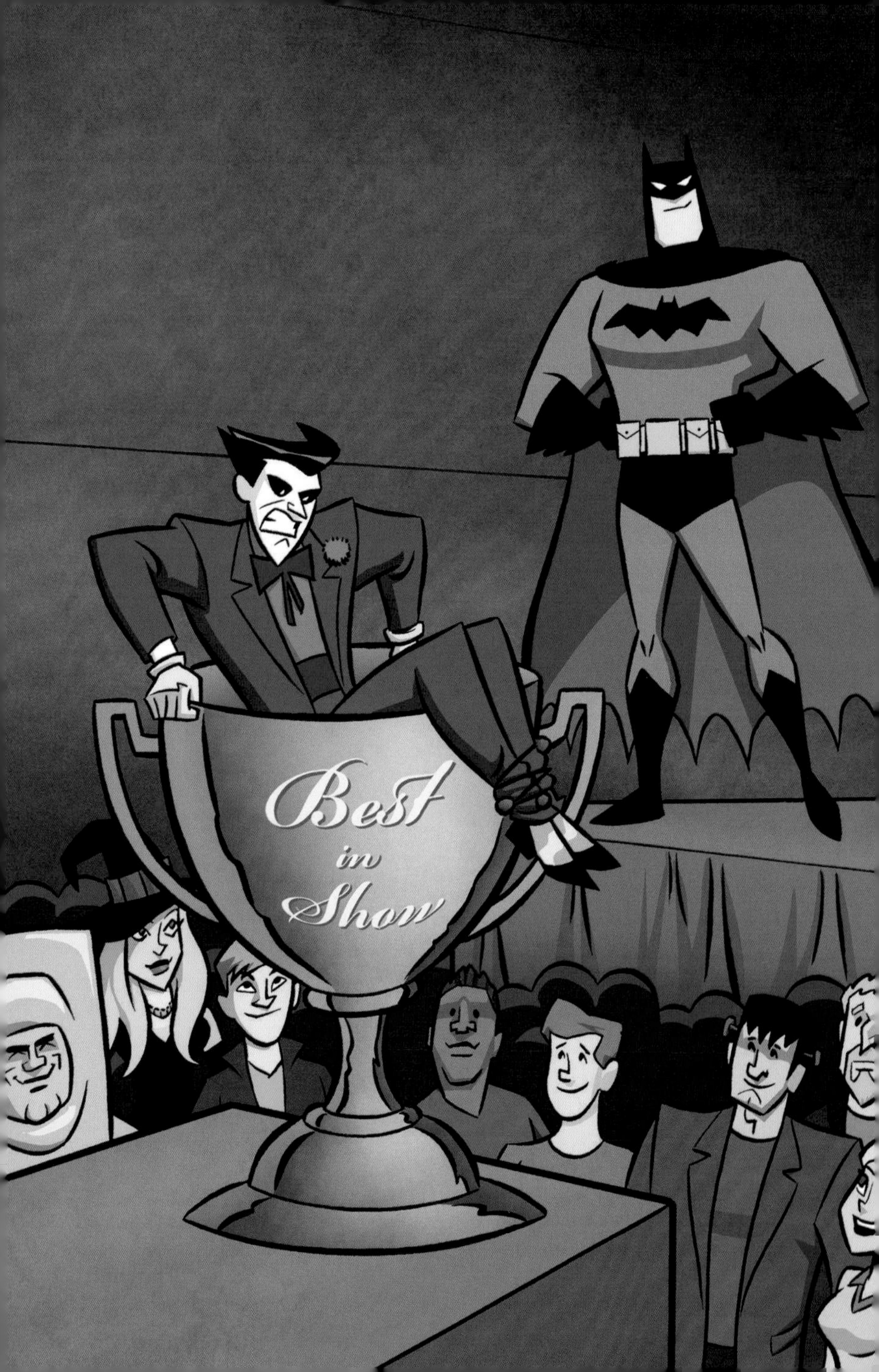
Best
in
Show

The Joker threatens to harm a hostage if Batman doesn't back off! The Joker breaks free of the bolo and gets to his feet.

"Stay back, or the lady gets it!" the Joker says.

Batman sees what the kooky criminal holds in his hand. It's a delicate statue of a Chinese goddess carved from jade.

"That's your hostage?" the Dark Knight says. "Don't make me laugh."

Batman knows that the object is priceless, but he won't let the Joker threaten him or the valuable antiquity.

"Besides, it's a replica," Batman bluffs.

"Oh well, in that case . . ." the Joker shrugs and tosses the statue over his shoulder.

The Dark Knight dives toward the artifact and catches it before it hits the floor. He rolls to his feet and carefully places the statue on a display stand.

"That wasn't a replica. That was real!" the Joker says, astonished. "You tricked me!"

"I made you give up your 'hostage,'" Batman replies.

"I have one more trick up my sleeve," the Clown Prince of Crime announces as he throws a smoke grenade. A stinky purple cloud fills the exhibit hall.

"You might have a trick up your sleeve, but I have an arsenal in my Utility Belt," Batman says as he puts on a gas mask. He pulls a small device from one of the compartments. The screen shows a red shadow fleeing the smoke-filled room. "I can follow your heat signal, Joker."

"All I need is a head start!" the Joker shouts.

Batman tracks the Joker through the exhibit halls. He can tell that the crazy criminal is running scared. There is no laughter. Suddenly, the thermal image of the Joker disappears from the heat-sensing device.

"The Joker has gone cold," Batman realizes. He stands in front of a door labeled Lunchroom, Employees Only. "Hmm, has he stopped for a snack?"

Turn the page.

Batman enters the room and examines it for evidence of the Joker. A scuff on the floor is the only clue he needs.

"It's time to play a joke on the Joker," Batman says to himself.

The Dark Knight makes a lot of noise as he opens cabinets and drawers and pretends to make himself a sandwich. He sits down at the lunch table and puts his feet on a chair.

"Chasing the Joker is exhausting. I need a snack," Batman announces in a loud voice. "I think I'll take a break for a while."

The Dark Knight starts to count down in his head. Ten, nine, eight . . . He gets to five when the refrigerator door opens, and the Joker scrambles out.

"Brrr! It was cold in there!" the criminal says.

"You're going to be 'on ice' in Arkham for a long time," Batman says as he puts Bat-cuffs on his foe.

THE END

To follow another path, turn to page 11.

The gladiators circle the Dark Knight. He remains still. He lets them make the first move.

One of the warriors strikes with a trident. The tip glows red with blazing laser light. Batman leans backward to avoid the searing jab. He uses his momentum to pivot on one heel and swing his other leg to knock down his opponent. **SPLAAAT!** The gladiator falls on his face.

"Booo!" the Joker jeers from his throne.

A second warrior approaches the Dark Knight holding a sword. The weapon looks ordinary until it shoots fire like a flamethrower! Batman dodges the fiery assault, but his cape does not. The fabric begins to burn.

"Yaaaay!" the Joker cheers. He pushes a button on his throne and the cardboard crowd cheers, too.

Batman ignores the flaming fabric and leaps toward the second gladiator. He lands a knockout punch on his opponent. The Dark Knight stands over his fallen foe and calmly pats out the sparks on his smoldering cape.

Turn the page.

"Fire-resistant fabric. It's standard on all my Batsuits," Batman explains.

The remaining gladiators drop their weapons and run away. They jump back down the hatch to escape having to battle Batman.

"Cowards!" the Joker yells after them.

The Clown Prince of Crime presses another button on the throne. A door opens at one end of the arena, and a giant robot strides out. It's an enormous replica of the Joker in gladiator armor.

"Let's see how you do against the Champion," Joker challenges.

The robot lumbers toward the Dark Knight. It swings a giant sword. Batman sprints between its ankles and lassos them with a Batrope. The mechanical warrior trips and falls. *BOOOOM!*

"See?" Batman says.

The Dark Knight picks up two of the weapons that the human gladiators dropped. He walks across the arena with a flame sword in one hand and a laser trident in another.

"Next," he points at the Joker.

The Joker gulps and runs. He abandons his hostage and his hyenas.

"It's every emperor for himself," the Joker says as he makes a break for it.

He does not get far.

A Batarang whirls through the air. It circles the Joker. Suddenly, a filament net pops out and drops over the fleeing felon. The Joker is tangled in its web and is stopped in his tracks.

"Thumbs down," the Joker grumbles as he squirms like a worm in the net.

Batman frees the hostage and leashes the hyenas. He walks over to the Joker and stands over the defeated criminal.

"I proclaim these gladiator games over," the Dark Knight declares.

THE END

To follow another path, turn to page 11.

"I thought I was the crazy one!" the Joker yelps as Batman dangles from his shoe. The parasail carries them toward the Ferris wheel.

"I hope you know how to drive this thing," the Dark Knight says.

"Heeheehee! I don't have a clue!" the Joker laughs hysterically. He looks down and sees the tense muscles of the Dark Knight's jaw. It makes him cackle even harder. "Oh, come on. Where's your sense of adventure?"

"We must have different definitions of that word," Batman replies as they crash into the Ferris wheel.

The parasail canopy tangles in the giant ride. The fabric twists and knots. The impact spins the Joker in the parasail cords while Batman hangs onto the villain's ankle with all his strength.

"Ow ow ow!" the Joker complains.

"A sore ankle is about to be the least of your worries," Batman warns.

SNAAAP! The parasail cords fray and break!

"Yaaaaa!" the Joker screams as they fall.

A Batrope launches from the Dark Knight's handheld launcher and wraps around a structural bar of the Ferris wheel. Batman and his foe come to a sudden stop in midair.

"Are you glad I have your ankle now?" Batman asks the Joker.

The super-villain is not so jolly as he watches the remains of the ruined parasail drop into the Gotham River. The swift current swallows the sail in a churning whirlpool.

"Help?" the Joker whimpers.

Batman stretches out a hand to aid his enemy.

"Sucker!" The Joker laughs.

A shock from the Joker's trick hand buzzer zaps through Batman's body. His fingers spasm and make him release his grip on the Joker.

The villain falls away from the Dark Knight and plummets toward the Gotham River. As a final act of madness, the Joker waves goodbye!

Turn to page 75.

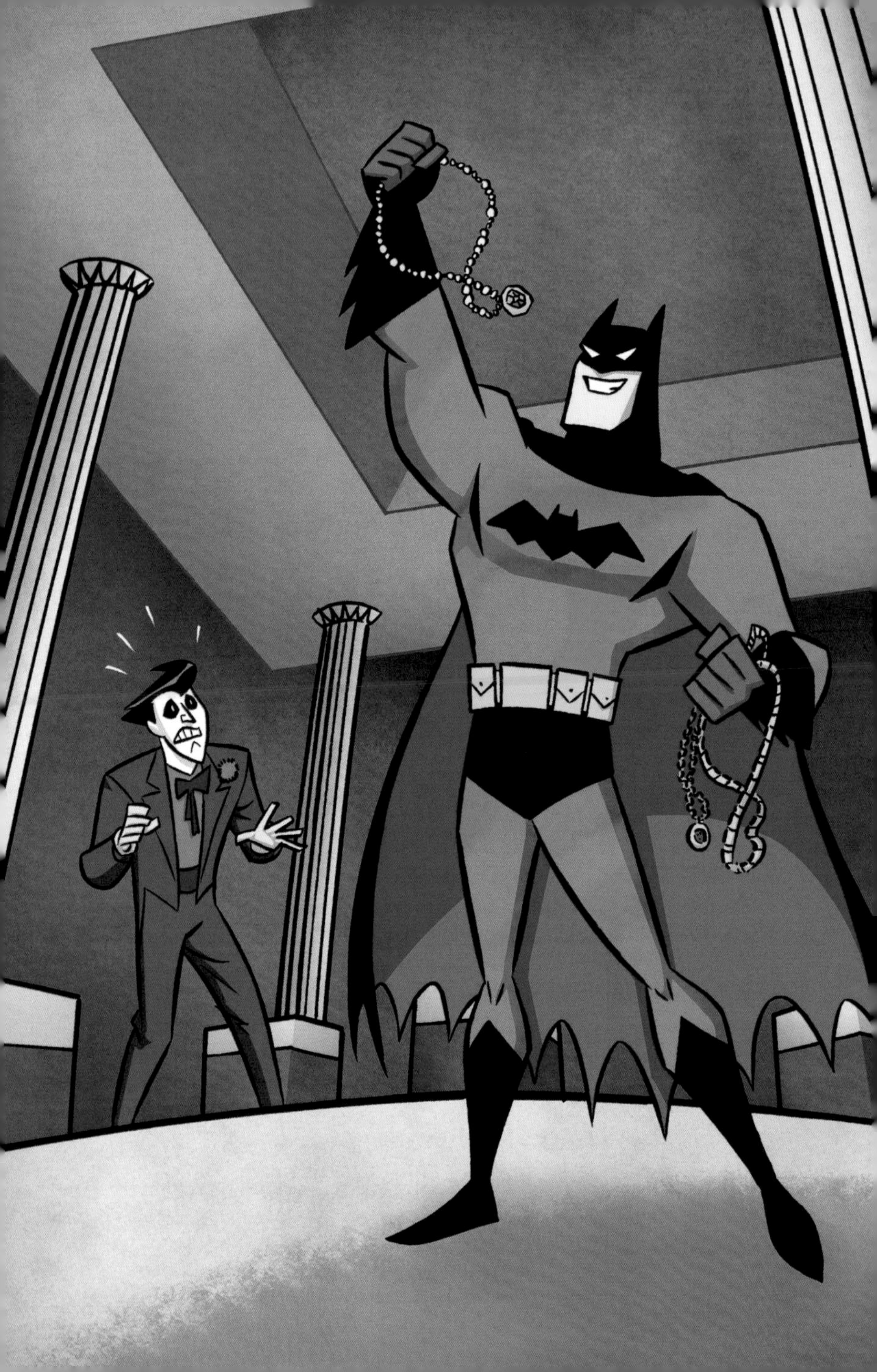

The Joker stares in disbelief at the sight of the Dark Knight's brightly striped uniform.

"You look more like a clown than I do," the Joker admits. "I love it!"

The Joker slaps his archenemy on the shoulder and lets out a hilarious laugh.

"Let's have some fun!" Batman howls maniacally. He rushes away from the Joker.

"Wait for me, buddy!" the criminal shouts.

The two new partners in crime raid the Egyptian exhibit hall. The Joker grabs a gold statue of a man with the head of a jackal.

"This is like a laughing hyena, right?" the Joker asks.

"Hee hee hee! That's Anubis, god of the dead," the Dark Knight chortles and snatches the statue from the Joker. "He's my kind of guy."

"You have a dark sense of humor," the Joker observes.

"You haven't seen anything yet," Batman says.

Turn the page.

The Joker drags a drop cloth from the painters' supply area and loads it with loot from the Egyptian exhibit. Batman removes his cape and fills it like a sack. They look at each other for a moment and compare their hauls.

"I got more than you did," Joker boasts.

"Quality, not quantity," Batman says.

"Hahahaha!" they laugh at each other.

Suddenly, the museum security alarm starts to blare. Lights flash. Metal gates begin to descend, blocking escape routes.

"Uh-oh! Time to run!" Batman laughs. He drops all of his stolen treasures and bolts.

The Joker tightens his hands around the edges of the drop cloth. He doesn't want to abandon his stolen statues and gems. The sight of rainbow Batman fleeing convinces the Joker that escape is a really good idea.

"He might be crazy, but he's not stupid," the Joker says.

He lets go of his loot and runs after Batman.

Turn to page 78.

Batman wrestles the claw from the jaws of the Joker's pet hyenas. They growl at the hero.

"Sit!" he commands.

The animals look at each other. They decide the tall, dark, human-with-a-cape is scary, and they run away.

Batman wipes off the hyena slobber from the dinosaur claw and examines the evidence. He illuminates the object with a multi-spectrum, high-intensity light from his Utility Belt.

"This isn't dinosaur skin. It's latex," the Dark Knight observes. "This is a movie prop."

The Joker may have gotten away for now, but he hasn't escaped the Dark Knight! Batman takes the claw to the Batmobile and places it on a sensor pad. The Batcomputer confirms its artificial content.

"Where was this made? List possible local sources," Batman instructs the computer.

"One location. The MWB Movie Studios," the computer responds.

Turn the page.

The movie studio is nearby the aquarium. When Batman drives onto the property he sees the Joker's pet hyenas running toward one of the soundstages.

"They're heading home to daddy," the Dark Knight concludes and accelerates in their direction.

Suddenly, pyrotechnics explode all around the Batmobile.

BOOOM! BLAAAM! Special effects bombs erupt in a planned pattern. The Dark Knight accelerates to escape the barrage. There is only one direction he can go. Batman speeds toward a dead end!

He can't avoid a crash. The Batmobile smashes into the side of a building — and through it!

WHAAAAM! The Dark Knight comes out on the other side of the wall. He is surprised to find himself in the middle of a chariot race!

Turn to page 82.

"Nooo!" Batman yells as he watches the Joker fall toward certain doom. "I tried to save you, you crazy clown . . ."

FWOOOOF! Suddenly, a small parachute deploys from a harness hidden under the Joker's jacket. The fabric fills with air and blossoms.

"Hohoho! Fooled you! I always keep 'em guessing!" the Joker howls as he floats away.

"I don't have to guess about where he's headed," Batman deduces as he calculates wind direction and speed on a handheld computer. The Dark Knight perches on the highest vantage point of the Ferris wheel. "He's going to the Gotham Zoo."

Batman does not need to see exactly where the Joker lands. He knows that the criminal always does something to attract attention. He doesn't have to wait very long before his prediction becomes truth.

A flock of bright parrots flaps into the sky. A pack of hyenas frolics through the zoo. An angry polar bear lumbers toward the penguin pond.

Turn the page.

The Dark Knight swings into action and swiftly reaches the zoo. Immediately, the hyenas rush at him.

"Hahaha! How do you like my new friends?" the Joker cackles from atop the animals' open enclosure.

Batman does not reply. He watches the canine creatures drool with anticipation. The pack begins to circle and surround the Dark Knight.

In a blur of motion, Batman reaches into his Utility Belt and pulls out a small capsule. He throws it to the ground between himself and the hyenas, and it erupts into clouds of thick smoke.

When the smoke clears, the animals are asleep on the ground, and Batman is on the roof of the enclosure. The Joker is gone.

"Hohoho! A swing and a miss!" the Joker taunts as he runs toward the penguin pond.

"The game's not over yet," Batman replies and races in pursuit.

The Joker hops over the fence surrounding the penguin pool and leaps across the rocks like a game of hopscotch. The penguins waddle away from the strange human.

A moment later Batman arrives at the pond but doesn't follow the Joker into the habitat. He stands outside the fence with his hands on his hips. He smiles. This disturbs the Joker more than being chased.

"What are you grinning at?" the prankster demands.

The Dark Knight points at the pool. The polar bear the Joker released swims in the water and circles the rock the trickster is standing on.

"Oops," the Joker gulps. "I guess the joke's on me."

"Game over," Batman declares.

THE END

To follow another path, turn to page 11.

The duo does not stop running until they arrive at the Joker's secret lair. It's hidden in an old warehouse on the Gotham River. The inside looks like a colorful carnival. Arcade games are scattered all over the room. A roller coaster run dominates the center of the hideout.

Batman looks around at his surroundings and begins to laugh. At first the Joker is offended.

"Hey! What's wrong with the place?" he asks.

"Nothing! It's great!" Batman howls. "I love the color scheme."

The Dark Knight waves a hand at his rainbow costume to prove his point. He trots over to one of the arcade games and starts playing.

BLOOOP! BLEEEP! DIIING! The sounds echo through the large lair. In a few minutes the machine announces a new winner.

"Whaaaat? You beat me!" the Joker gasps as he looks at Batman's score.

"Woo-hoo! I win! I win!" Batman celebrates.

The Jeering Jester is not feeling so cheery.

Turn to page 80.

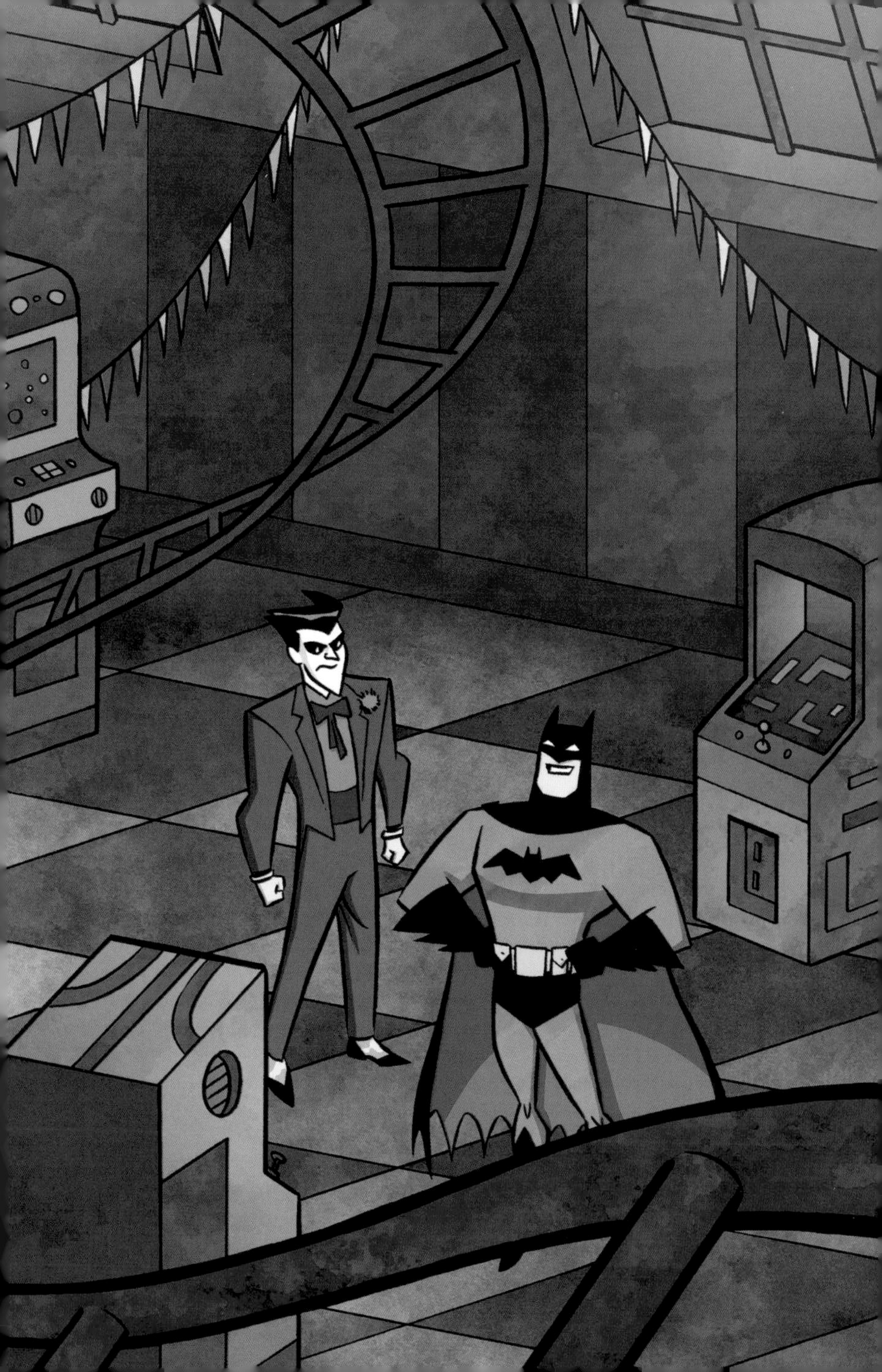

Batman flops down on one of the expensive couches. "Who's your decorator?" he gripes. "I have softer rocks in the Batcave."

"Those are genuine leather. I stole them myself!" the Joker grumbles.

Batman jumps up from the couch and heads to the kitchen area. He grabs pots and pans and clangs the cookware on the stove. Savory smells drift up.

"Oooh! What's cooking?" the Joker asks.

"It's a secret recipe." Batman laughs.

"Um, maybe I should be suspicious about the ingredients," the Joker gulps.

"I'm insulted!" Batman declares. He eats a spoonful of what he is cooking. Suddenly, his lips pucker, and he shakes his head.

Batman drops the spoon back into the cooking pot. His expression is serious as he turns around and faces the Joker.

"I'm back to normal now. My recipe was a cure for your laughing gas," Batman reveals.

"I'm so depressed," the Joker confesses. "We were a great team."

The Joker makes a run for it, but Batman snares his foe with a Batrope. Suddenly, police swarm into the hideout. Commissioner Gordon walks up to Batman.

"We followed your tracking signal from the Gem Museum. Your plan worked," Gordon says. "Sniff! Sniff! Something smells great!"

The police commissioner leans over the cooking pot simmering on the stove and starts to take a taste. A Batarang knocks Gordon's hand away from the bubbling liquid.

"That's for the Hazmat Team," Batman advises.

"But you ate it!" the Joker shouts as he is put into the Arkham transport.

"It was the only way to test my formula," Batman says. "Now I'll need antacids for a week."

THE END

To follow another path, turn to page 11.

Batman crashes the Batmobile through the wall of a movie soundstage, and suddenly sees that he's in the center of a Roman chariot race. Galloping horses are all around him.

"This is an interesting comparison of the term *horsepower*," the Dark Knight observes as he brings all the power of the Batmobile's mighty engine into action.

The vehicle roars. **VROOOOMM!** Batman steers the Batmobile through the crowd of chariots as accurately as he did through the bomb barrage. The agile automobile swerves and curves like a football player headed for a winning touchdown.

It takes the Dark Knight almost a full lap around the track before he finds the exit. He escapes the chariot racecourse, drives through a dim tunnel and out onto the set of a monster movie. A giant Tyrannosaurus rex looms in front of the Batmobile. Batman notices that the creature has only one hand.

"It looks like the Joker's hyenas were using it as their chew toy," the Dark Knight observes.

Suddenly, a small missile spirals through the air and blows up the T. rex prop. **BLAAAM!**

Batman swerves the Batmobile to avoid the flying debris and comes bumper-to-toe with a giant battle robot. A smoking missile launcher on its shoulder reveals the source of the dinosaur's destruction. One of the gun barrels swivels and points at the Batmobile.

"Activate emergency smoke screen," Batman instructs the computer.

Turn to page 85.

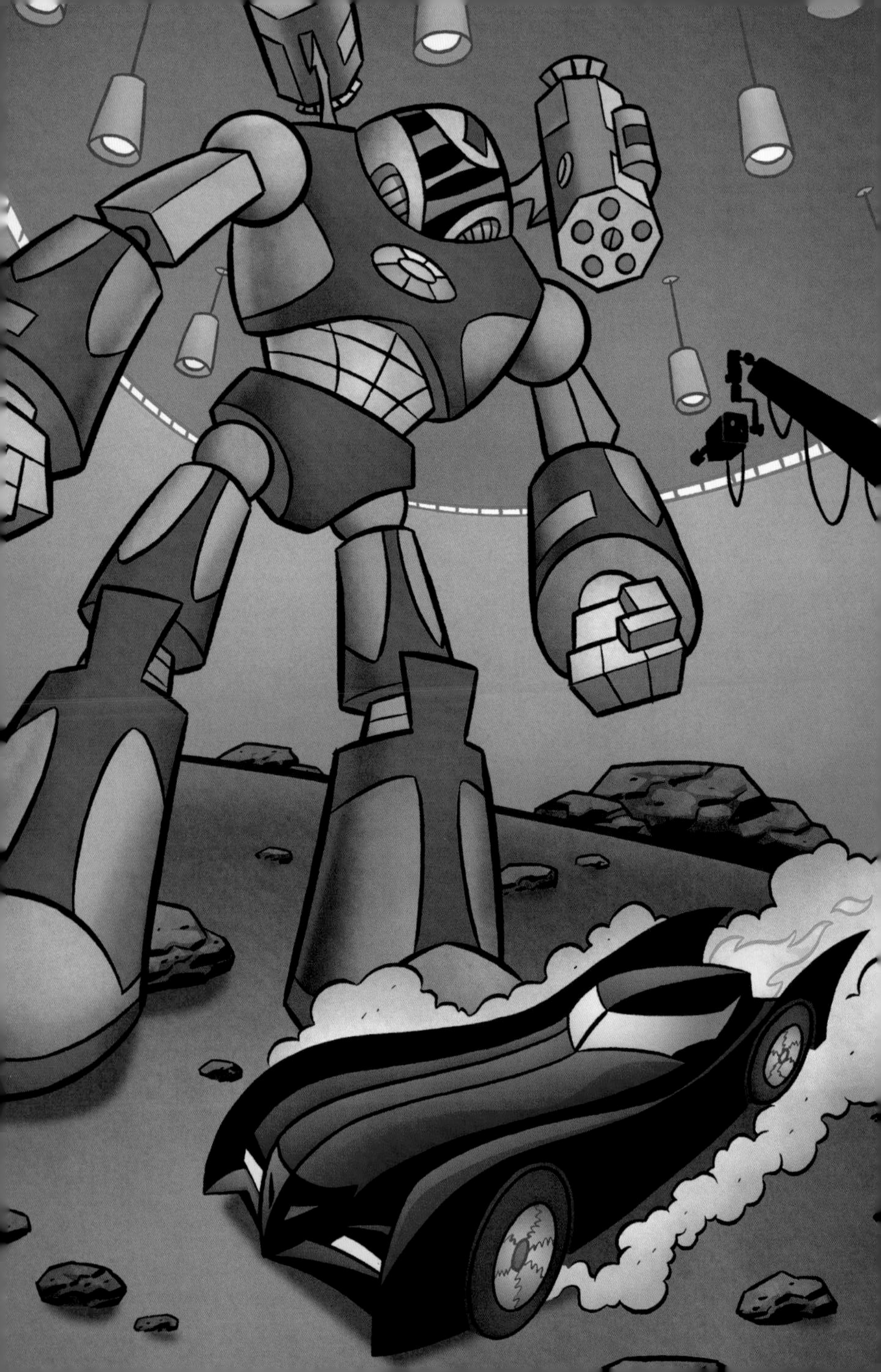

Clouds of black vapor erupt all around the Batmobile. Batman puts the vehicle in reverse and backs away just as the robot fires a missile.

BLAAAM!

When the smoke clears the robot is flat on the ground. It is missing a foot. Batman hops out of the Batmobile and walks over to the prone machine.

"It looks like you shot yourself in the foot," the Dark Knight observes. "Just like I wanted you to do."

Batman opens a hatch in the head of the robot and pulls the Joker out of the machine's control cockpit.

"It's time for you to go back to Arkham, Joker. You'll never make it in the movies," Batman declares.

THE END

To follow another path, turn to page 11.

"Hey! No hitchhikers allowed," the Joker says as he uses his free foot to stomp on Batman's fingers. The jerky movements make the parasail veer closer to the Ferris wheel.

"Look out!" the Dark Knight warns.

"Oh, don't be so afraid," the Joker says.

Batman twists his body and shifts his weight, forcing the parasail to swing away from the danger. A gust of wind lifts them higher into the air where a strong breeze takes them slowly down the river.

"You know, it's kind of pretty up here," the Joker says, gazing at the lights of Gotham City in the night. He starts to point out landmarks like a tour guide.

Batman looks at the same sights in a different way. He searches for the nearest building to attach a Batrope and pull them to safety. The parasail drifts over the middle of the Gotham River, and the shore is just beyond the reach of the launcher's range.

Batman knows he can't wait for another unpredictable gust of wind to drive them toward the riverbank. He climbs up the Joker's body until he can reach the control cords.

Batman grabs the strings and steers the parasail toward the city skyline.

"You're such a backseat driver," the Joker grumbles as Batman precisely pilots the parasail.

A giant replica of a candy cane looms in front of them on the top of a building. Batman aims for a landing on the roof, but the Joker suddenly tugs at the control strings. They swerve toward the symbol for the King Candy Factory.

Batman struggles to guide the parasail away from a crash landing. The Joker struggles to make it happen. Without warning the Jeering Jester unhooks his harness and drops.

"They say it isn't the fall that kills you," the Joker declares. "It's the landing!"

Batman hangs from the control cords and watches the Joker plunge toward certain doom.

Turn the page.

Even though the Joker is Batman's enemy, the Dark Knight will not let him perish. The hero launches a Batrope toward the falling felon.

SMAAAASH! The Joker crashes through a skylight window in the roof of the King Candy Factory. **ZWIIIP!** The Batrope zooms after him through the opening and into darkness.

The Batrope does not tighten. Batman knows that the Joker's weight is not on the end of the line. The Dark Knight retracts the rope, hoping to see that he is wrong for once. The Batrope zips back into the launcher — empty.

"I tried to save you," Batman says.

The Dark Knight lands the parasail on the roof of the candy factory. He walks over to the broken skylight and feels frustrated with his failure to keep the crazy criminal from destruction.

"Hohoho heehee hahaha!" Insane laughter swirls up from the blackness inside the building.

"He's alive!" Batman realizes.

Turn to page 96.

It's no laughing matter to the Joker as he watches Batman steal gems and jewelry from the museum displays. The Dark Knight is painted as brightly as a tropical parrot and acts like a loony bird. Seeing his enemy behaving like him makes the Joker jealous.

"Batman is stealing my act," the Joker says.

The Joker decides to put a stop to the Dark Knight's bad behavior. He takes a deck of special playing cards out of his pocket and throws them at the crazy crime fighter. The weighted cards knock the loot from Batman's hands.

"Ha ha ha! Hey!" Batman complains between fits of uncontrollable laughter.

The Dark Knight grabs a Batarang from his Utility Belt and throws it at the Joker. He is laughing so hard that he misses.

"Let's play a game!" Batman howls. He shoves the Joker in the chest. "Tag! You're it!"

The Joker falls backward as the Dark Knight runs out of the exhibit hall.

Turn the page.

"Ow, he plays rough," the Joker mutters as he gets to his feet and rubs his rear end.

The sound of Batman's hysterical laughter leads the Joker to the Egyptian hall of the Gotham Gem Museum. When he arrives, he sees the Dark Knight climbing into a golden sarcophagus. The heavy lid slams shut, but the Joker can still hear Batman laughing inside the coffin.

"Now where is that masked menace?" the Joker says in a loud voice. He pretends that he doesn't know where Batman is hiding.

The Joker makes a noisy show of searching the exhibit hall. Suddenly, he pounces on the sarcophagus and opens the lid.

"Aha! I've got you—" the Joker starts to say. He stops when he sees that the coffin is empty. He scratches his head in confusion. "How'd he do that?"

POW! A fist smacks the Joker in the jaw. Batman pops up out of the sarcophagus like a clown out of a jack-in-the-box.

A shiny fabric drops to the floor.

"Hahaha! I got you! And you're still 'it'!" Batman cackles as he gallops away on an imaginary horse.

"He might be crazy, but he's crazy like a fox," the Joker admits. "He covered himself with a mirror shroud. It created the illusion that the coffin was empty. Nice trick. I've got to remember that one."

The Jeering Jester sprints through several exhibit halls in pursuit of the deranged Dark Knight. After several minutes of running, he has to stop and catch his breath.

"Whew! I'm in worse shape than I thought," the Joker gasps. "I really should exercise more. Ha! Who am I kidding?"

The pooped prankster limps over to a bench. He plops down and sighs like a deflating balloon.

"This is why that caped creep always wins. He wears me down. Note to self: get a Joker Car!" the Joker pants.

Turn to page 99.

Batman lassos the dinosaur digit with a Batrope and snatches it from the jaws of the hyenas. When they see the Dark Knight they whimper and run away.

Batman examines the claw and sees that it's made of soft plastic and has a manufacturer's serial number stamped on the side. Batman enters the numbers into his portable Batcomputer terminal and views the results.

"Tony's Toy Company. Ten Tons of Fun for Everyone," Batman reads aloud. "The Joker is probably using the place as a hideout."

The Dark Knight calls up a map to the factory and hops into the Batmobile. When he arrives at the building a few minutes later it looks deserted, but he knows that looks can be deceiving.

Batman goes inside to investigate. Giant, ten-foot toys fill the main space. There are stuffed teddy bears, unicorns, and a T. rex dinosaur with one arm.

"It looks like I found the hyenas' chew toy," Batman observes.

Suddenly, the teddy bears growl. The unicorns stampede. The T. rex roars. The toys have come to life!

Batman knows that even though the playthings are soft and full of stuffing, they are huge and could hurt him. There is only one thing for him to do.

Batman runs toward the thundering unicorns! He leaps like a trick rider at a rodeo and lands on the back of one of the unicorns. Suddenly, he is part of the herd. He uses his weight to steer the unicorn back toward the teddy bears. The herd follows and they slam into the bears.

Batman jumps off just before the impact.

BWOOOMP! The stuffed animals bounce off each other. Batman lands on the tummy of one of the teddy bears and uses it like a trampoline.

SPROING! He springs into the air.

The Dark Knight comes down on the shoulders of the one-armed dinosaur.

Turn to page 95.

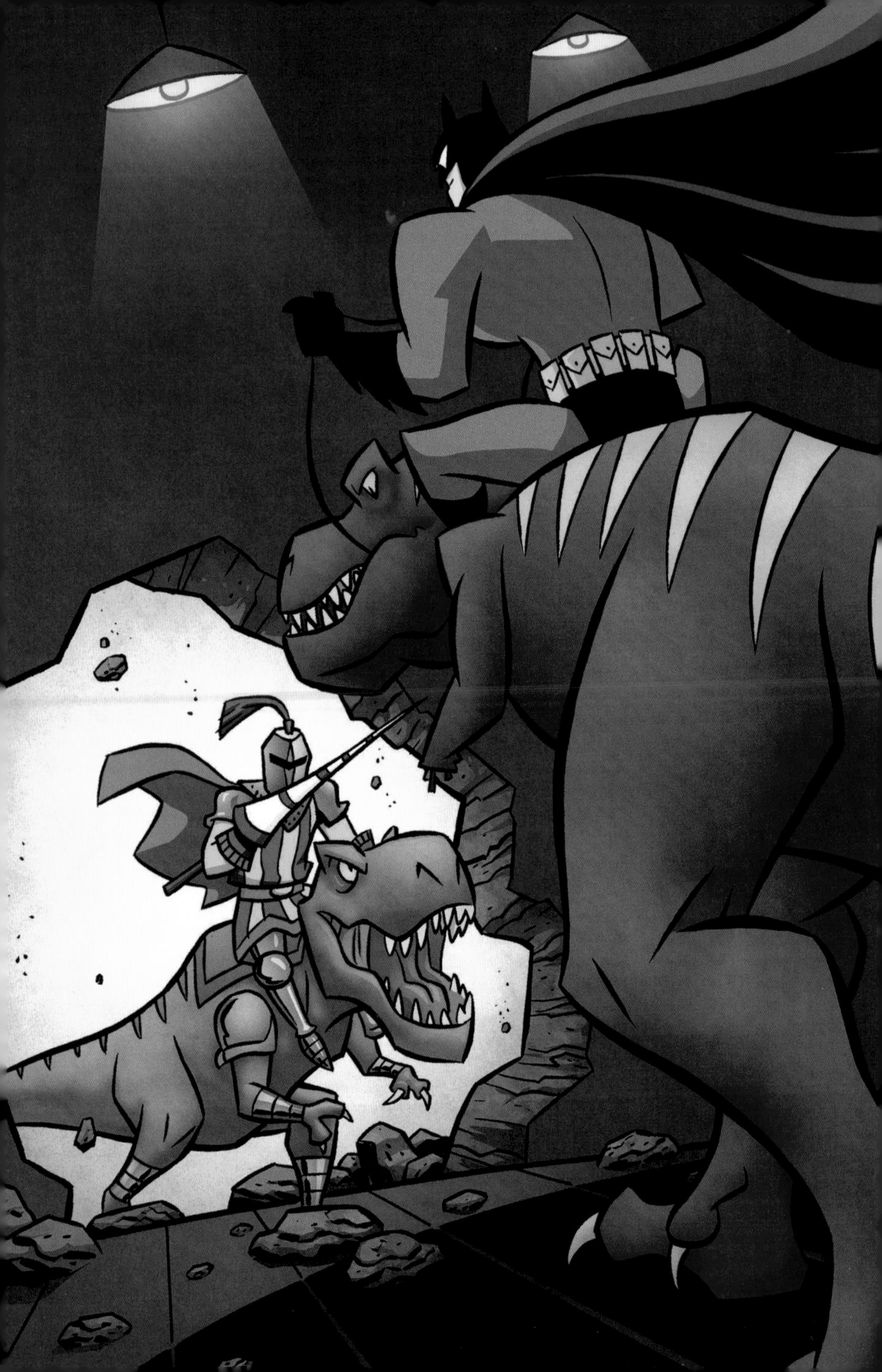

"It looks like I've traded in one bronco for another," Batman says as he ties a Batrope around the dinosaur's head like a bridle and reins. "Giddyap."

The dinosaur obeys and lumbers forward. Batman rides the giant toy through the factory looking for the Joker. He knows that the Joker must be controlling the animated animals from somewhere in the building.

Suddenly there is a crashing sound as a wall collapses. When the dust clears Batman sees another giant T. rex dinosaur thump through the rubble. It is covered in armor like a medieval knight, and so is its rider.

"Joker!" Batman says.

"Hail, and well met, Dark Knight! Let's joust!" the Joker challenges.

The Jeering Jester urges his saurian steed forward. He points a lance at Batman and rushes headlong toward his opponent.

Turn to page 103.

The Dark Knight follows the sound of the Joker's laugh into the King Candy Factory. He jumps down through the smashed skylight and lands in the middle of the company showroom. Massive, shadowy objects loom in the dark room.

Batman pulls a small halogen flashlight from his Utility Belt and sweeps the room. Giant mascots and candy replicas fill the showroom. They are a history of the King Candy Company.

When Batman sees the collection, he is taken back in memory. He is no longer the Dark Knight but Bruce Wayne as a child. He remembers the sweet swirl of the candy canes, the enormous size of the sour balls, and the ultra-sticky taffy.

"Hohohoho! Do bats like sweets?" the Joker howls as he pushes a mascot statue toward the Dark Knight.

Batman snaps out of his memories and into reality. He leaps to one side and rolls out of the path of the statue. **CRAAAASH!** The mascot shatters.

"Hee! I didn't think so!" The Joker cackles.

The Dark Knight fires a Batrope toward the felon's fleeing shadow. The rope narrowly misses and retracts into the launcher.

Batman follows the Joker's trail of laughter out of the showroom and down into the factory level of the building. The Dark Knight does not hesitate at the sight of giant machinery blending boiling ingredients. He leaps through the maze of mixers in pursuit of his candy-colored foe.

"Let's stir things up!" the Joker laughs as he flips a master switch and the entire factory goes full speed.

The Joker watches Batman balance on top of a bubbling batch of sugar that is about to become sour balls. He howls with mirth when the cauldron tips and the Dark Knight vanishes from sight.

ZWIIIP! PIIING! The Batrope shoots out and anchors into the factory ceiling. The Joker's smile turns upside down and into a frown when he sees the Dark Knight ascend from danger. He turns and runs!

Turn the page.

Batman disconnects from the Batrope and lands on the factory floor. A quick glance reveals the Joker's sugary footprints. The trail leads Batman to the taffy division of the factory. When the Dark Knight arrives he sees a line of giant paddles stirring rows of massive vats.

Suddenly, a blob of taffy hits Batman!

"Heeheehee!" the Joker chortles.

"Go ahead, give me your best shot," Batman challenges. He stands still and spreads out his arms, offering the Joker a perfect target.

The super-villain can't resist. He plunges his hands into the taffy vat all the way up to the elbows to get a giant handful.

"Uh-oh," the Joker gulps. His hands are stuck. "You tricked me!"

"I guess I get the last laugh," Batman declares.

THE END

To follow another path, turn to page 11.

"Okay! I quit!" the Joker announces suddenly. He staggers to his exhausted feet and limps out of the exhibit hall. "You win, Batman! Gotham City can say goodbye to this Clown Prince."

The Joker walks slowly through the Gem Museum. He acts as if he is making a final pilgrimage. He gazes at the precious stones in the display cases and wipes away tears.

"Sniff! I'll miss trying to steal you, Star Diamond. So long, King Opal and Queen Ruby," the Joker whimpers sadly.

"Boo-hoo-hoo!" Batman sobs and comes out of the shadows. His mask is wet with tears. "I'm sorry, Joker! I didn't mean to hurt your feelings!"

The Dark Knight stretches his arms wide and runs toward the Joker to give him a hug.

"Uh, you're hurting my ribs..." the Joker wheezes as Batman embraces him.

"We should be partners!" the Dark Knight declares. "We should be pals!"

"Uh-oh," the Joker gulps.

Turn the page.

A few minutes later the Joker swings from a Batrope. His new best friend swings next to him. The streets of Gotham City are a blur beneath their feet.

"Why couldn't we use the Batmobile?" the Joker yells as the night air whips past his face.

"You said you wanted to get more exercise," Batman replies.

"I was talking to myself. Hey! Were you listening?" the Joker asks angrily.

"Hahaha! My cowl gives me the hearing of a bat, remember?" Batman laughs.

"I'm the Clown Prince of Crime! Get me down from here!" Joker demands.

"Your wish is my command, your majesty," Batman says.

The Dark Knight cuts the Batrope, and the Joker falls toward the street pavement.

"Not what I meannnttt!" the Joker corrects his statement as he plunges toward certain doom.

Turn to page 102.

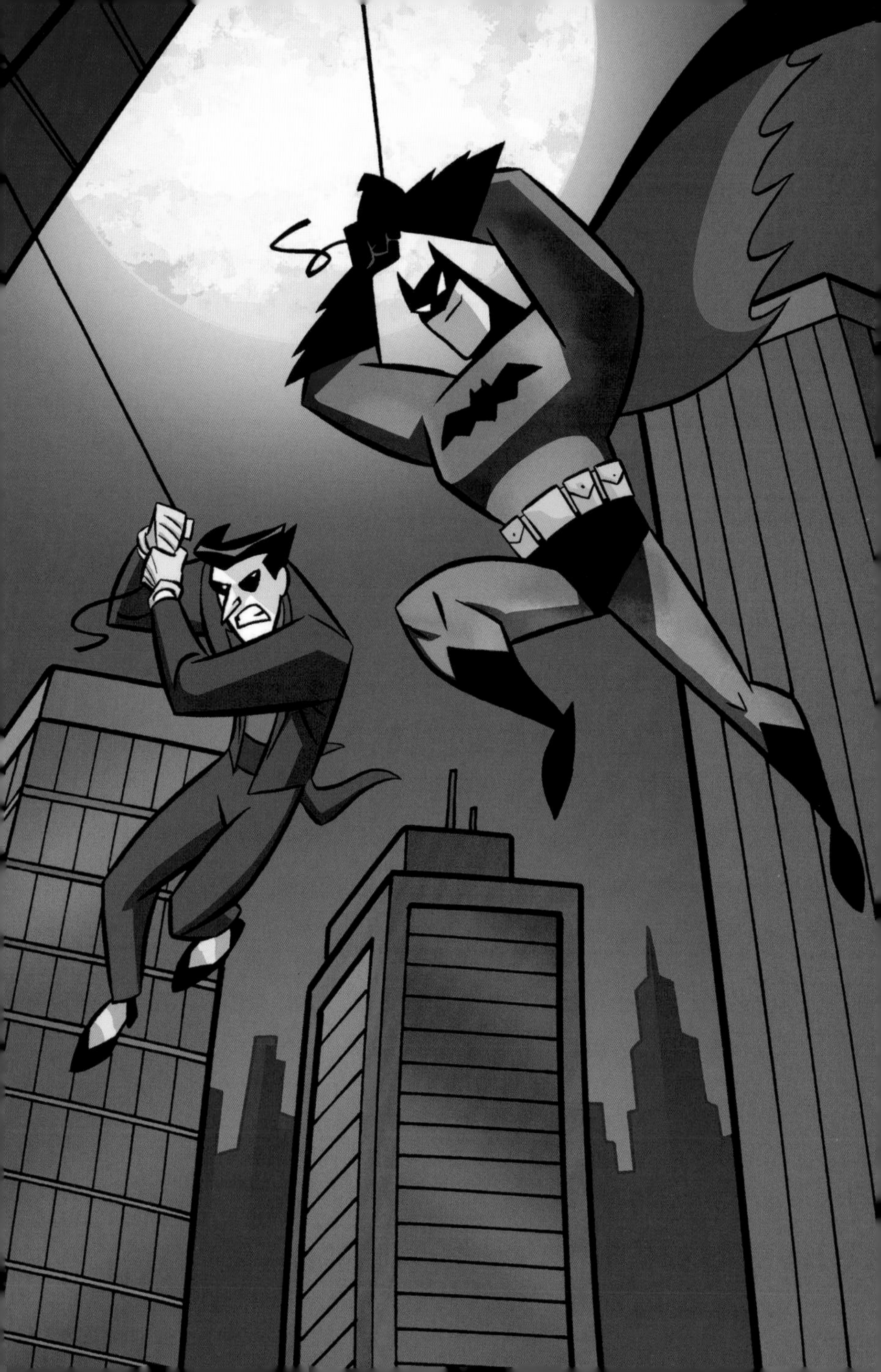

Suddenly, a net catches the Joker in midair. It's attached to a parachute, and the Joker floats gently to the ground.

"You said you wanted to take the Batmobile!" Batman cackles from the cockpit of his vehicle. The Joker hops inside.

"Step on it!" the Joker howls.

The Dark Knight guns the powerful engine. It roars like a wild animal ready to spring into action! In the next second the Joker has Bat-cuffs on his wrists. He stares at Batman in surprise.

"I was never affected by the laughing gas," Batman reveals. "I used nose filters from my Utility Belt and then pretended to be loony to lure you here."

Police cars surround the Batmobile. As the Joker is taken into custody he declares: "I told you there can be only one Joker in Gotham!"

"And there will always be a Batman," the Dark Knight replies.

THE END

To follow another path, turn to page 11.

"I know he's crazy, but this is nuts," the Dark Knight admits as the Joker races toward him on a giant armored dinosaur.

Batman dodges the jousting lance as the Joker thumps past him on his mechanical mount. ***WHUMP! WHUMP! WHUMP!*** The Dark Knight reaches out and snatches the lance from the Joker's grip. He flips it in the air and grabs the hilt. It is now in his control.

"Hey! That's not in the rules!" the Joker complains. Then he erupts with laughter. "Hahaha! What am I saying? There are no rules!"

The Joker pushes a button on his dinosaur's armor. Huge flames shoot out from its mouth!

"Hoohoo! How about some Flame Action?" the Joker cackles gleefully. His dinosaur steed spouts fire like a dragon as it advances toward the Dark Knight.

The tip of Batman's jousting lance starts to burn like a candle. It burns down to the handle in a few seconds.

Turn the page.

The Dark Knight drops the lance and searches around his mechanical dinosaur for tricks he can use against the Joker. There are no activation buttons. He shrugs as if giving up.

"Hahaha! Have at thee!" the Joker shouts.

"You sound like an old movie," Batman says. "Let me add some modern sound effects."

The Dark Knight pulls a single Batarang from his Utility Belt and throws it at his foe. It misses the Joker and whirls away.

"Ha, ha, you missed me!" the Joker jeers.

The Batarang returns and hits the Joker's dinosaur on the armor between its eyes.

CLAAANGANGANG! The metal plates vibrate and create an echo. The mechanical creature starts to shake.

"Wha-wha-waww!" the Joker stammers as his mount rattles and quakes under him. Pieces of its armor break apart and fall to the ground.

"Sonic Shock Batarang," the Dark Knight explains. "It's an essential piece of my arsenal."

The sound waves from the Batarang unhinge the Joker's giant armored dinosaur. Its metal bolts pop, and it starts to fall apart under him.

"Playtime is over," the Dark Knight declares.

Batman swings his dinosaur around so that its tail smashes through the Joker's crumbling mount. What's left of the toy shatters. Pieces go flying in every direction. So does the Joker.

The Joker lands on a conveyor belt. He laughs as it carries him away from the Dark Knight.

"Hahaha! See you later, alligator!" Joker says.

Batman doesn't make a move to chase his foe. He sees something the Joker does not. Suddenly a giant nozzle sprays the Joker with foam. Another one covers him with stuffing. A moment later he is zipped up into the shell of a giant stuffed animal. Batman waits at the end of the toy factory's assembly line for the Joker.

"All wrapped up and ready for a padded cell at Arkham," the Dark Knight observes.

THE END

To follow another path, turn to page 11.

AUTHOR

Laurie S. Sutton has read comics since she was a kid. She grew up to become an editor for Marvel, DC Comics, Starblaze, and Tekno Comics. She has written Adam Strange for DC, Star Trek: Voyager for Marvel, plus Star Trek: Deep Space Nine and Witch Hunter for Malibu Comics. There are long boxes of comics in her closet where there should be clothing and shoes. Laurie has lived all over the world. She currently resides in Florida.

ILLUSTRATOR

Ethen Beaver is a professional comic book artist from Modesto, California. His best-known works for DC Comics include Justice League Unlimited and Legion of Superheroes in the 31st Century. He has also illustrated for other top publishers, including Marvel, Dark Horse, and Abrams.

GLOSSARY

abducted (ab-DUK-tuhd)—kidnapped or taken

asylum (uh-SYE-luhm)—a hospital for people who are mentally ill and cannot live independently

gladiator (GLAD-ee-ay-tur)—a warrior of ancient Rome who fought against other warriors for entertainment

hostage (HOSS-tij)—someone taken and held prisoner as a way of demanding money or other conditions

hyena (hye-EE-nuh)—a wild animal that looks somewhat like a dog and has a shrieking howl

illuminate (i-LOO-muh-nate)—to light something up

investigate (in-VESS-tuh-gate)—find out as much as possible about something

lapel (luh-PEL)—the part of a collar of a coat or jacket that folds back over itself

replica (REP-luh-kuh)—an exact copy of something, especially a copy made on a smaller scale than the original

sarcophagus (sar-KAWF-uh-gus)—a stone coffin

THE JOKER

Real Name:
Unknown

Occupation:
Professional Criminal

Base:
Gotham City

Height:
6 feet 5 inches

Weight:
192 pounds

Eyes:
Green

Hair:
Green

The Clown Prince of Crime. The Ace of Knaves. Batman's most dangerous enemy is known by many names, but he answers to no one. After falling into a vat of toxic waste, this once lowly criminal was transformed into an evil madman. The chemical bath bleached his skin, dyed his hair green, and peeled back his lips into a permanent grin. Since then, the Joker has only one purpose in life... to destroy Batman. In the meantime, however, he's happy tormenting the good people of Gotham City.

- The Joker always wants the last laugh. To get it, he's devised dozens of deadly clown tricks. He has even gone as far as faking his own death!

- Always the trickster, the Joker designs all of his weapons to look comical in order to conceal their true danger. This trickery usually gets a chuckle or two from his foes, giving the Joker an opportunity to strike first.

- The Clown Prince of Crime has spent more time in Arkham Asylum than any Gotham criminal. But that doesn't mean he's comfortable behind bars. He has also escaped more times than anyone.

- While at Arkham, the Joker met Dr. Harleen Quinzel. She fell madly in love and aided the crazy clown in his many escapes. Soon, she turned to a life of crime herself, as the evil jester Harley Quinn.

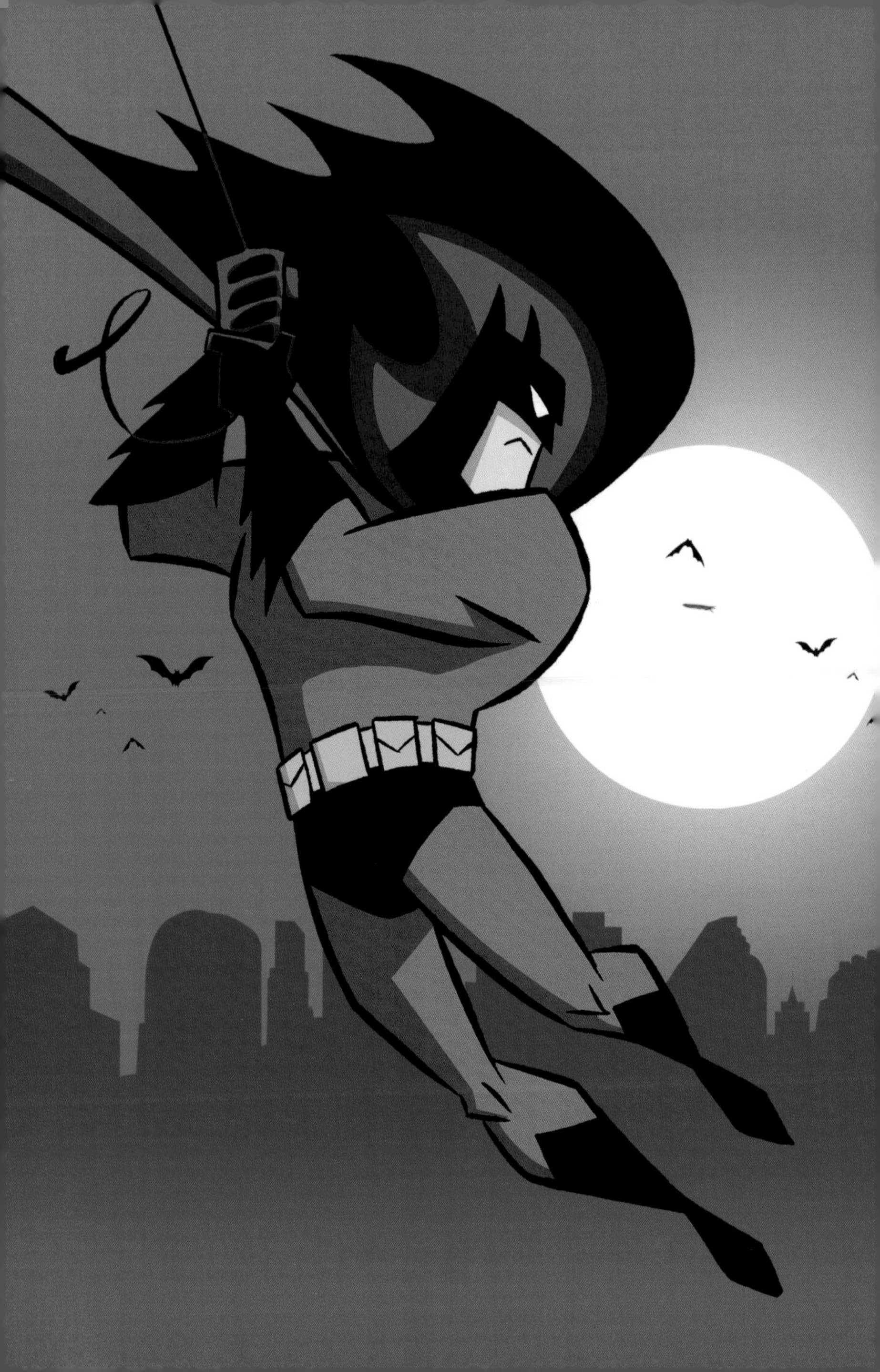

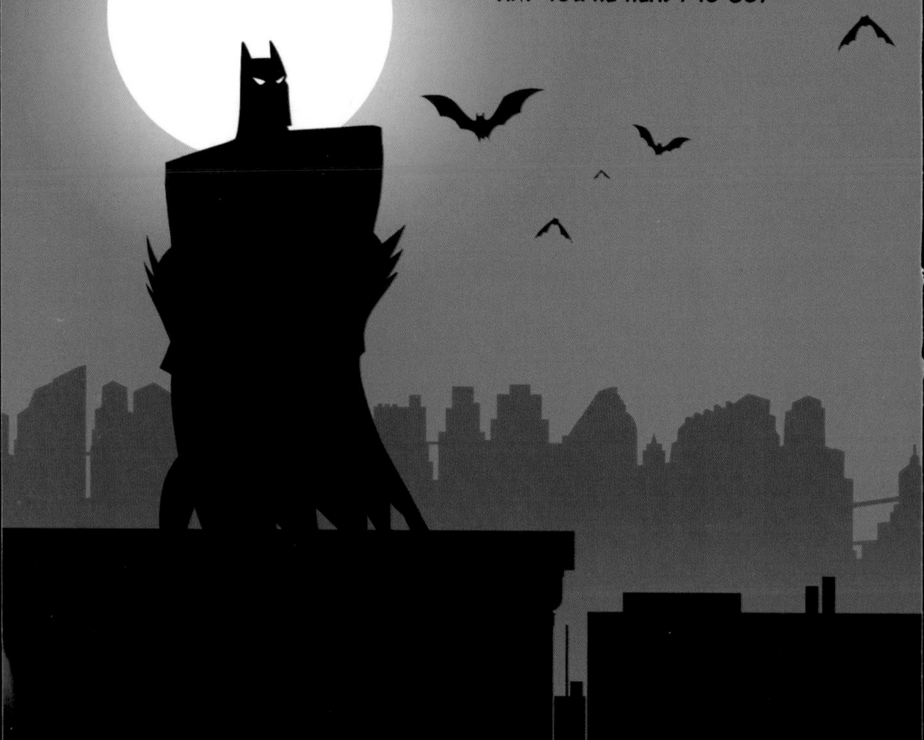

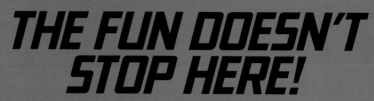